FLIRT WITH ME

A WITH ME IN SEATTLE NOVEL

KRISTEN PROBY

AMPERSAND PUBLISHING, INC.

Flirt With Me
A With Me In Seattle Novel
By

Kristen Proby

FLIRT WITH ME

A With Me In Seattle Novel

Kristen Proby

Copyright © 2021 by Kristen Proby

All Rights Reserved. This book may not be reproduced, scanned, or distributed in any printed or electronic form without permission from the author. Please do not participate in or encourage piracy of copyrighted materials in violation of the author's rights. All characters and storylines are the property of the author and your support and respect are appreciated. The characters and events portrayed in this book are fictitious. Any similarity to real persons, living or dead, is coincidental and not intended by the author.

Cover Design: By Hang Le

Cover photo: Wander Aguiar

Published by Ampersand Publishing, Inc.

Paperback ISBN: 978-1-63350-108-9

CHAPTER 1

~HUNTER~

Someone once told me that life gets easier as you get older. That as your children age, you settle into a nice rhythm in the day-to-day, worry less, enjoy more.

Whoever said that is a fucking liar. Or never had kids.

I've been a single dad for fifteen years. Not once in that time has it been easy.

"Where the hell is she?" I mutter as I finally sit for the evening, ready to enjoy a beer and a basketball game.

Rachel, the apple of my eye, said she'd be at her friend Kyla's house for the night. But when I open the app on my phone to track *her* phone—an app she doesn't know I added to her device—it tells me that she's not at Kyla's house at all.

"Maybe they went for ice cream." I sigh, already

sure in my gut that they didn't just innocently go out for dessert.

Rachel's always been a good girl, but since she hit puberty a couple of years ago, she's made it her mission in life to test my patience.

Hell, I retired from fighting so I could be around more, gone less. Sure, at thirty-six, my body was starting to suffer from the constant poundings, but fighting is all I know. I've been in the ring since I was younger than my daughter.

It's not about the millions of dollars that come in from every fight, or the sponsorships. I don't give a rat's ass about the attention or celebrity—much to my publicist's dismay.

It's about the rush of being in that ring with another man, the skill it takes to outwit and outmatch him.

Training for and being in the ring is my drug.

But age and responsibilities dictated that I walk away. That, and the very real possibility that it could kill me.

Fucking head injuries.

If it weren't for Rachel, I would have continued fighting until I died in the ring.

The only thing I love more than the sport is my daughter. She's the priority. She used to come with me when I traveled and then stayed behind with my parents when it became too much for her, and she needed to be in school.

But now *she's* too much for my parents, and I can't have a kid who's getting into trouble.

I don't want her to be like me.

So, as I stare at the blinking red dot on my phone and will it to move, I sigh.

I need to go find my daughter.

I set the untouched beer on the kitchen counter, grab my keys, and leave my Seattle home in search of the one person on this planet that makes me want to yank my hair out.

According to the map, she's about ten miles from home, in a neighborhood that I know is residential. And when I slow my Rolls Royce in front of the brownstone, I scowl.

It looks like something out of an eighties movie. A whole bunch of cars line the street, and the music coming from the building can probably be heard all the way downtown at the Space Needle.

The fact that there aren't cops here is shocking.

I double-park the car, and when I climb out, I point to a kid who's leaning against his Honda, trying to charm a girl.

"You."

He looks my way. "Yeah?"

"See this car?"

His eyes widen when he glances at my sleek, black Rolls. "Yeah. Nice ride, dude."

"If even *one* speck of dust is on it when I come out

of that house, you're the one I'm going to kill for it. Got it?"

"Sure." He swallows and then narrows his eyes at me. "Hey, you're Hunter Meyers. The fighter."

"That's right. And if anyone dicks with my car, we'll have a problem."

He just nods. "I'll keep an eye out."

"Good."

It's a hot summer night in Seattle. The windows of the house are wide-open. Along with the blaring hip-hop music leaking out, there are laughs and cheers, a girl's squeals.

They're having a hell of a time.

I'm going to kill her.

I stalk right inside, my eyes narrowed and scanning the sea of kids. Jesus, nobody here can be over the age of seventeen. Red Solo cups litter every surface, and I'm immediately taken back to my misspent youth.

But this time, it's my *daughter*, and I know what happens at parties like this.

Hell, no.

I move quickly, skimming faces. No Rachel.

But when I glance down, the red dot is still here, at this location.

She has to be here.

I climb the stairs and start opening doors. Thankfully, the rooms are empty. I haven't seen anyone losing their virginity.

But when I open the door at the end of the hallway

and flip on the light, my worst fears are on full display, right before me.

"Oh, my God." Rachel's face pales as I see red. "Dad, what are you doing here?"

"You. Shut it." I glare at her and turn my wrath on Derek, the *nineteen*-year-old kid from the gym I practically live at. The same gym Rachel comes to after school. "You'll meet me at the gym at eight a.m., or I'll come find you."

I take Rachel's hand and pull her up off the bed. Thank Jesus and all the saints she's still clothed.

They were making out, and Derek's hand had made its way up her shirt, but he didn't get past second base.

If he had, he'd be bleeding right now.

"Dad, this is so embarrassing."

"Good."

I pull her down the stairs, through the house, and outside.

A small group of boys stands around my car. No one's touching it, but they're looking.

I can't blame them. It's a hell of a ride.

"Get the fuck out of my way," I growl, and the sea of boys parts for us.

I open the passenger side and wait for my pissed-off daughter to sit, and then I walk around the hood of the car, find the kid I spoke to when I parked, and pass him a bill.

"Good job."

I get behind the wheel as the kid stammers and stares at the hundred in his hand and then drive off.

"I can't believe this," Rachel mutters.

"That makes two of us." I drag my hand down my face and glance her way. Her arms are crossed over her belly, her shoulders sagging. She's *pouting*. "Are you seriously pouting because I caught you in a lie, tracked you down, and pulled your ass out of there before you did something monumentally stupid with that asshole, Derek?"

"He's *not* an asshole," she retorts in anger. "I wasn't drinking or doing drugs. I just wanted to be with my friends."

"Should you get an award for not drinking or doing drugs when you're not supposed to be doing those things anyway?"

"You don't understand."

Oh, but I do. "I've been your age—"

"Yeah, and I've never been yours," she says before I can finish.

God, I love that she's strong-willed.

And it pisses me right off.

"We can't do this, Rach." My voice is quiet now. Getting riled up and raising my voice doesn't help anything. I want her to *hear* me. "You're fifteen. I've already retired so I can be with you more. We have a great home. You go to a good school. Grams and Gramps are nearby, ready to help us out at a moment's notice. And yet you *still* pull this shit. So, I guess we're moving."

She spins in the seat and stares at me in horror. *"What?"*

"I'm done. I can't just lock you in your room all the time. I can't just take everything away. Your friends here are shit. And if the changes I've already made haven't helped, then something else has to give because right now I feel like we're both constantly being punished."

"No, I don't want to move."

"Yeah, well, I don't want a daughter who does whatever the fuck she wants, despite what I say. So, here we are. We need a change of pace."

Rachel shakes her head. "I can't believe you're doing this to me."

I don't reply to her as I grab my phone and call the non-emergency line for the police department.

"Yeah, I need to report a party with underage drinking."

I WALK through the doors of Sound Fitness at just before eight the next morning. I already dropped Rachel off at school.

She's not speaking to me.

I can live with that.

The dude that had his lips and hands all over my

kid last night is a young fighter who's been hanging around the gym for the past couple of years. He has an attitude, but most of us do.

The attitude isn't what bothers me.

I wave at the owner, Ben, and breeze back to the locker room, where I change clothes, grab the tape for my hands, and walk back out to the ring that sits in the middle of the space.

I've been using this ring for training for more than twenty years. The previous owner, Rich McKenna, is the reason I'm not in jail and instead fell in love with fighting.

His son, Nate, is my friend.

Those at this gym are my family.

I like that Ben made improvements but didn't change the atmosphere, the *vibe* of the place. It's my second home.

When I approach the ring, I see Derek walking through the door.

I knew he'd come.

He's asked me for help with his training in the past. I'm about to train him on a life lesson.

One he won't soon forget.

"You wanted to see me?" He raises his chin defiantly.

"Get in the ring."

He frowns. "I'm not dressed—"

"Get in the motherfucking ring."

I duck under the ropes and drop my head from side

to side then stretch my back. When he stands on the platform, I move in.

"Hey!" His hands come up, and fear fills his eyes. "I don't want to fight you."

"No?" I walk around him. I want to keep him guessing on what I might do next.

And I need to move away so I don't just rip his throat out.

"Nah, I thought you wanted to talk about last night."

"Oh, I do." I grin—a humorless, toothy smile. "How old are you now, Derek?"

"Nineteen." He puffs up his chest.

"And do you know how old my daughter is?"

He fumbles for a second but then shrugs. "Fifteen, I guess."

"Fifteen." I bounce on my toes. "Do you make a habit of messing around with underage girls?"

"Look, man, it wasn't like that. She came on to me."

"Wrong answer." I spin and hit him in the chin with my elbow, but I don't hit him hard.

I want him to stay conscious.

"Fuck!" He cups his chin. "Jesus, Hunter."

"That's Mr. Meyers to you," I reply. "My daughter is a minor. You are an adult. In what universe did you think it was okay to put your hands on her?"

"Listen—"

"If you give me more shit about her coming on to you, you won't walk out of here today."

He swallows hard and rethinks. "I like her. She's hot. And funny."

"I'm going to give you some advice. You're always asking me for it, so here it is. Are you listening?"

He nods and keeps his eyes on mine.

"Don't fuck around with *any* underage girls. Ever. It'll only get you into trouble. Keep your head in the ring. Keep your dick in your pants. If your dick happens to make its way out of your pants, make sure she's over the age of fucking *consent*. Do you want to end up in jail?"

"No."

"Do you want me to kill you?"

His eyes widen. "No."

"Because that's what's going to happen if I find out that you've even so much as *looked* at Rachel again. She's too young for you, D."

"Yeah." He sighs and pushes his hand through his blond hair. "Yeah, okay. Look, I'm sorry, okay? I just like her."

"I like junk food, and I can't have that, either." I get close to him so only he can hear. We've lured in quite the crowd. "Touch her again, and you'll regret it. I promise you that."

"I got it."

I nod and walk away from him, confident that I've just solved *that* problem.

Now, to work on the next.

I make my way to the locker room and change

again. I'd normally spend a few hours here at the gym, working out and training, but I need to set some things in motion.

I've just grabbed my bag when Nate walks through the door and grins when he sees me.

"Been a while," he says and shakes my hand. "That last fight in Vegas was a damn good one, man. I'm sorry I missed it."

"Thanks." The *last* fight. I still haven't quite wrapped my head around it.

"What are you up to now?"

"Finding a place to move with Rachel. She's been getting into trouble, hanging with kids she shouldn't. I just had to shake down Derek because I caught him with his hands on her last night."

Nate's eyebrows shoot up. "What the fuck?"

"Yeah, exactly. It's time I move her out of the city."

"Where are you thinking of going?"

I blow out a breath. "I'm not sure. I want a smaller town for her, a slower pace. But I don't want to go too far. My parents are here and not getting any younger, you know?"

"Yeah, I get it." Nate nods. "Julianne has family on a little island nearby. It's just a ferry ride away. It's a nice place, definitely what you described. You should check it out."

"If it's that close, I'll look into it. Maybe I'll find a nice place on the water. Enjoy the quiet for a while."

"That's how you know you're getting old. When the peace and quiet looks appealing."

I snort. "I've had nothing but chaos for my entire adult life. I'll take the quiet. Rachel's going to stay with my parents for a few days. I think I'll check out this island."

"I'll text you the details. Keep me posted on it."

"Will do. Thanks."

I leave the locker room with a new purpose.

Looks like I'm headed to the beach.

WITH RACHEL safely tucked away with my parents, I made my way over on the ferry last night and checked into the vacation rental I reserved online.

Rachel still isn't speaking to me and has been pretty mellow since the other night, so I trust that she won't give Mom and Dad a hard time.

I plan to be here for two days to look at some property and get a feel for the place. I did some research. The schools are ranked well, there's little to no crime, and it seems to be a pretty laid-back place.

I would never have considered a small town when I was younger. I wanted the action, the fast pace of the city.

But this is what's best for Rachel and me. And, so far, I like what I see.

A small village with a few restaurants, shops, and

cafés. There's a pub that reminds me of many I visited when I was in Ireland, and I'm headed that way for dinner.

The neighborhoods are well kept and nice. There are some beautiful homes for sale on the cliffs overlooking the ocean, and I have an appointment with a realtor to look at several tomorrow.

I push my way into O'Callaghan's Pub and feel the grin spread over my face. It's as if someone picked up a pub from Ireland and slapped it down right here in Washington.

I make my way through the people seated at tables, listening to the musicians playing on the small stage in the corner, and find an empty stool at the bar.

I sit and turn to take it all in.

There's dancing and drinking, and plenty of food.

It smells like heaven.

"And what is it I can do for you?"

I turn at the Irish accent and find a man, roughly my age, waiting behind the bar.

"A Guinness," I say. "And a menu."

"Coming up," he replies as he passes me a menu and reaches for a clean glass to start building my drink. "So, tell me. What is Hunter Meyers doing in my pub?"

I grin. "I'm in town for a couple of days, looking around. I'm a fan of Irish pubs, so if the food is as good as it is across the pond, I'll probably be in here every day."

"It's better." He winks at me and pushes the glass my way.

I order the chicken wings and fries, plan to run an extra two miles tomorrow, and sit back to enjoy the show. A few people glance my way, but no one really pays me any mind, and I relax.

I don't mind talking with fans, but it's also nice to feel a little anonymous, to just sit back and enjoy.

Three waitresses make their way through the busy bar. Two redheads and a blonde.

The blonde looks familiar, but I can't place her.

Suddenly, both of the redheads—they must be sisters—jump up on the stage and start singing with the band, a lively Irish number that I've heard a few times before.

But never quite like this.

When the one with the darker auburn hair laughs and jumps down off the stage to heft her tray and make her way to the bar, I feel my stomach tighten.

That thick hair is tied up in a messy pile on the top of her head. Her green eyes shine as she laughs and chats with her customers, making her way toward me, weaving through tables and bodies.

She has an hourglass figure with a tiny waist, but hips and tits that would make the gods weep. And when she glances my way, and those Irish eyes meet mine, my world tilts on its axis.

"You're new," she says playfully, with a wink. "But I

see my brother set you up already with a Guinness. Did you order food?"

"I did."

She nods. "If he slacks off, give me a wave and I'll help you out."

"Here's to hoping he slacks off." I grin at her, pleased when that smile spreads easily over her gorgeous face. "Nothing against your brother, he seems like a nice guy, but I'd much rather have the attention of a gorgeous woman."

"My sisters are around here somewhere."

I laugh and shake my head. "You. I'd rather it were *you*."

"Well, isn't it handy then that I'll be here all night?"

And with that, she's off and running again.

I sip my beer, enjoying the atmosphere of O'Callaghan's. My eyes keep drifting back to the gorgeous redhead with the greenest eyes I've ever seen. I've been too busy lately to take much interest in a woman. I have plenty on my plate as it is.

But there's something about *this* woman that's grabbed my interest.

"You went for the wings," she says as she delivers my food. She sets the basket in front of me and nods toward it with a smile. "A good choice."

"What's your favorite thing on the menu?"

"The stew." She winks, and then she's gone again, but I notice, as I eat, that she lets her gaze wander my way as she hustles back and forth between her tables.

I'm surprised when I take my first bite of dinner. The bartender was right. It's better than I've had before.

"Need anything?" My waitress asks and props her hands on her hips, which only makes her T-shirt stretch enticingly over her breasts. "More napkins? Another beer? My phone number?"

I laugh, but I find myself nodding. "I'll take all three."

"Coming right up." She winks and hurries behind the bar to pass me napkins. "Keegan, this handsome man needs another beer."

She pulls one of the napkins off the top and jots down her number, then passes it to me.

"I'm not one for handing out my number," she says and tucks a stray hair behind her ear. "Just to make that clear."

"Why me?" I fold the napkin without even glancing at it and tuck it in my jeans. I fully intend to use it while I'm here.

But instead of answering, she just winks and gives me a sassy grin, then she's off to check on her tables.

Yes, the island looks promising.

CHAPTER 2

~MAEVE~

Someone is licking my toes.

I turn in the bed and pull off my sleeping mask, open one eye, and stare down into big brown eyes.

"Murphy." I sigh and squint at the clock. "It's only nine in the morning, you know."

Murphy lets out a whine and rests his chin on the bed.

"Yeah, yeah, I know. You want breakfast."

I yawn and sit up, stretching before stepping into my soft slippers.

Murphy is my eldest brother's big yellow dog. When Kane and his wife, Anastasia, are out of town, one of the siblings keeps the dog.

Kane and Anastasia are in San Francisco this week for a museum opening featuring some of my big brother's work. I'm damn proud of him.

And, I'm happy to have Murphy around. He's good company.

"But you get me up too early when I've closed down the pub the night before." I scratch his ears and lead him to the kitchen.

I open the back door so he can run out and do his business while I scoop him some food and get to work on coffee for myself.

I enjoy working evenings at O'Callaghan's for my brother, Keegan. The pub's been in our family since I was little—when my parents moved to America from Ireland and opened the bar here on our little island. Keegan bought it from Ma and Da a handful of years ago so the parents could retire and split their time between Washington and our little Irish village near Galway.

Helping out is fun, and I'm happy to do it. Especially when something unexpected happens like last night. I don't think I've ever flirted that much with a customer. I know for a fact that I've never given my phone number out to anyone. I kept asking myself all night what in the world I was thinking, but then I'd swing by the stranger, and he'd smile in that ridiculously sexy way, and I had zero regrets.

None.

So, yeah, the pub can be lots of fun.

But, Jesus, it's hard to have two completely different sets of responsibilities.

I might moonlight as a waitress, but my first love is

real estate. I've been selling homes on the island for several years. I like showing properties and helping people find the places they want to call home.

And it's a good thing that Murphy woke me because I have an appointment with a new client at ten-thirty. I'm showing him three homes today, all on the water.

This client must have quite a bit of money. Which doesn't hurt my feelings because that means the commission will be a good one.

I like my little house, but I've been saving up for my dream home. It just came on the market, and this new client could be my ticket to that purchase if I find the house for him, and the commission is high enough.

I open the door for the dog, and as he eats, I sip my coffee and nibble on some toast, then make my way upstairs to get ready for the day.

My real estate clothes are far different from my pub attire. In the evenings, I'm in jeans and T-shirts, my hair tied up, and I usually leave looking disheveled, covered in something, and smelling like beer and French fries.

But during the day, for showings and closings, I'm in a shift dress, heels, and my hair is down around my shoulders, the curls tamed as much as they can be.

I apply my makeup with a light hand, wanting to be cool and professional. When I'm all ready to go, I smile down at Murphy who's been watching every move I make.

"I think we're ready to go. You're going to go hang out with Shawn and Lexi today, okay?"

Murphy's mouth drops open in a doggie grin.

"Let's go."

We make our way out to the car, and I drive over to the house on the cliffs that I sold to Shawn a couple of years ago, not long before he met his wife, Lexi. My brother and Lexi are both writers and work from home, so Murphy can hang out with them while I'm busy.

"Good morning," Shawn says as he steps outside to meet us. "And hello to you, boy."

He rubs Murphy's side and watches me with those steady green eyes.

Out of all of us siblings, Shawn is the quiet one. The most logical.

And, sometimes, he sees too damn much.

"You look tired."

I narrow my eyes at him. "That's a nice way of saying I look like shit."

"If I thought you looked like shit, I'd say so. Didn't sleep well?"

"Do I ever?" I shrug. "Insomnia is a bitch. I closed the pub last night and sat up doing some research for a new client until about five. Murphy here woke me at nine, but it's good he did because I'm meeting said client in a few minutes."

"Do you work tonight?"

I flash a grin. "Of course. It's the weekend, Shawn. Are you and Lexi going to man the kitchen?"

"Of course," he echoes. "It's the weekend. I'll see you later, then."

He waves and ushers Murphy into the house.

The pub is a family affair. We all do our part.

I check the time and the address of the first home I'm showing, and realize I'm running just a smidge late.

I hate that.

I need to get there first so I can open the place, turn on all the lights, and make sure it's ready to show.

I've shown this first house to several couples. It's on a nice piece of property at the tip of the island, but the interior needs a little updating. I encouraged the sellers to do just that, but they're not interested. They just want to unload it.

So, I'll keep showing it until someone decides they want a project.

To my relief, I'm the first to arrive and hurry through the house, flipping on lights and opening doors and windows to let in some fresh air. The doorbell rings, and when I reach the front door, I open it to a tall, muscly man with light brown hair, a scruffy chin, and a cocky grin.

"Oh, hi." I clear my throat and look a little closer, then feel my face flush with embarrassment. "It's you. From the pub last night."

"I was about to say the same thing." He slowly looks

me up and down, taking in every inch of me. From the interest in his brown eyes, I'd say he likes everything that he sees, and his gaze sets my pulse to hammering and makes me swallow. Hard.

"You must be Hunter Meyers."

He raises a brow. "I am."

"I'm Maeve O'Callaghan, the realtor." I hold out my hand to shake his, surprised by the strength in his grasp and the little zing that passes between us. "I guess we never got around to exchanging names last night. Come on in."

He steps in behind me as I walk ahead.

"This is the first house we'll see today. I have two others lined up."

"I found another online last night," he says. When I glance back, I notice that he's not checking out the house. His eyes are on *me*. "Is there any way I can see it tomorrow?"

"Sure, I just have to give the seller twenty-four hours' notice. Which one is it?"

I turn to him and watch as he taps his phone. I'm so close to him, I can feel the heat coming off of him. I touched him a few times last night—just a hand on his shoulder. I laughed and flirted like it was going out of style.

And he's my freaking *client*.

I'm horrified.

Hunter turns his phone to me. "This one."

My stomach sinks when I turn my attention to his screen.

It's *my* house.

"I'll just make a call when we're finished here." I try to smile at him and then gesture to the living space we're currently standing in. "Go ahead and have a look around the house. I'm here if you have any questions."

"Thanks."

I give him space to wander around and take in the views, check out the rooms.

"The view is one of the best on the island," I say as he returns to the living space.

"It's a good view, but the house isn't my style." He shoves his hands in his pockets and watches me with interest.

I want to climb him like a tree.

But I'm *working*.

"It could be, with some TLC and sweat."

He smirks. "I'm not handy when it comes to home improvements. I think I'd rather have something more move-in ready."

I nod, not surprised.

That seems to be everyone's response to this house.

"Okay, do you want to follow me to the next one?"

"First, I want to address the elephant in the room."

I raise an eyebrow.

"Last night."

I clear my throat and look down, but he reaches

over and taps my chin, making me look him in the face again.

"Why are you embarrassed?" he asks.

"Because I was way too flirty last night. If I'd known you were my client, I wouldn't have behaved that way. I know it was mostly harmless, but—"

"Have I given you the impression that I thought you were inappropriate last night?"

I bite my lip and frown when his eyes narrow on my mouth. "No. You haven't."

"Good. Because I had a good time. And I'm reminded that I was a little rude if I didn't introduce myself to you and ask for your name."

"I wrote it on the napkin I gave you," I reply.

"I haven't looked at it yet," he confesses. "I was going to call you later after I looked at houses."

I tilt my head to the side. "You were?"

"Yes. And I still might. But first thing's first." He gestures for me to lead the way. "After you."

"You go ahead. I have to turn off lights and lock up real quick."

"I can help with that."

Before I can decline the offer, Hunter hurries through the house with me, buttoning it up so we can move on to the next property.

I lock the front door and turn to him. "Okay, I think we're ready to move on."

"I'll be right behind you."

I pause when I see the vehicle he's driving. The gorgeous, flashy car.

"Is that a Rolls Royce?"

He flashes that smile again. "Yeah."

"May I ask what you do for a living, Mr. Meyers?"

The smile leaves his face, and he stares at me with skepticism. "You don't know?"

I shake my head. "Should I?"

"The bartender…he knew."

"Well, given that my brother and I don't share a brain—and thank God for that little mercy—I can say that I'm not aware of who you are. Aside from Hunter Meyers from Seattle. And you drive a Rolls. Oh, and you like chicken wings. And you flirt with waitresses."

His lips twitch now. "I don't always flirt with waitresses. I was a mixed martial arts fighter until recently."

"That explains the muscles." The words are out of my mouth before I can stop them, but Hunter doesn't seem to mind.

He laughs and then nods. "I guess so. Noticed the muscles, did you?"

"I mean, they look like they're going to bust through that T-shirt."

His grin widens, and he crosses his arms over his chest, making the muscles even more prominent.

I'm not blind. I'm a red-blooded woman. Hunter is hot with a capital H. The kind of hot that melts panties and makes a girl daydream about things.

"I'm fascinated by whatever is going through your head right now," he says, clearly enjoying himself.

If I don't move us along, I'll drag him inside and have my way with him.

"Let's just go look at the other houses."

I turn my back on him and get into my car, starting it up. When he's done the same, I pull out of the driveway and head toward house number two.

On the way there, I call the realtor representing *my* dream house and set up a showing for tomorrow. Then, I quickly Google my client, just so I'm not completely blind, and continue to make a fool of myself.

Well, of course, Keegan knew who he was. Keegan watches all of those fights. Even plays them in the pub. But I don't really pay attention. Still, Keegan should have said something. He saw me flirt with the man. Aren't brothers supposed to *say* something?

We pull up to the next house, and I get out of my car, trying not to fidget when I feel Hunter stand close behind me as I unlock the front door.

"All of the homes you're interested in have great views of the water," I inform him as we walk inside. "This one also has a pool, which is heated and in a pool house because of the cold weather here."

I tell him all about the many great things the property has to offer and then let him explore. Out of all of the homes I'll be showing him, this is the largest.

It's a lot of house for one person.

Especially when it's a vacation house.

But, I learned a long time ago not to judge.

"Okay, this isn't bad," he says when he returns to the kitchen a few minutes later. "I like the pool, but I'm not crazy about where the master suite is. No water view."

"You could change it," I suggest. "Convert the two bedrooms that face the water into a master suite. Or, you could add a brand-new addition onto the main level down here with great views."

"True." He nods thoughtfully, looking around the space. "Okay, this stays on the list."

"Great." Hope takes root in my chest that he won't choose the house that *I* want. I'm so close to buying it, I can taste it. "We have one more on our list for today."

"And then you should have dinner with me tonight," he says smoothly.

"I don't usually date clients." I cringe and shake my head. "I *really* should have asked for your name last night."

"I didn't ask you on a date," he counters and walks out of the house ahead of me. "It's just dinner. We can discuss house buying and call it a business meeting. See? Not a date at all."

I raise a brow and lock the door behind us. "What a clever offer. Unfortunately, I can't have dinner with you. *Or* a meeting. I'm busy tonight."

His eyes narrow. "Are you already taken?"

"I beg your pardon?"

That cocky grin flashes again and makes my stomach clench.

Damn it, he's sexy. Potent. Dangerous.

"You can beg all you want," he murmurs, and then seems to shake himself out of his thoughts. "Are you attached to someone?"

I tilt my head. "You know, that's a rather archaic way of asking me if I have someone in my life, Mr. Meyers."

"Hunter."

"I don't have a boyfriend, no. Not married. I definitely wouldn't have flirted with you the way I did last night if I were in a relationship. That's just…gross."

"Agreed." He leans over and brushes his fingertip over my cheek, then comes away with an eyelash. "Blow."

"Blow?"

"Yeah, you blow it away and make a wish."

I pucker my lips and blow, and then laugh a little. "This is crazy."

"Which part?"

"The whole situation. I'm not afraid to admit that I'm so far out of my comfort zone, I'm not sure where it went."

"Comfort zones are overrated." He winks. "I just wanted to make sure I wasn't poaching on someone else's territory. I'm a lot of things, but I'm not that. We haven't known each other very long, but I like flirting with you, Maeve."

Yeah, well, the feeling is entirely mutual.

"Let's move on to the other house," I suggest, and climb into my car.

Good God, he's potent. I've never had a client who had such an impact on my hormones. It's unsettling. And ridiculous.

But it's also kind of fun.

What's the harm in a few mild flirtations? It spices up the day. He's charming, sexy, and I haven't had anyone in my life to flirt with in longer than I care to remember.

I just have to remember that he *is* a client, and I have to maintain my professionalism.

After that brief pep talk, we pull into the driveway of the last house for the day. I can't help but admire the sleek lines of his fancy car or the way he looks when he steps out of it—tousled hair and dark aviators on his face, highlighting his square jaw.

And those muscles…

I've read about men who just pick up women and have their way with them, moving them about to suit their needs and desires. I can't say I've ever had that life experience.

But it's something to daydream about.

"Keep looking at me like that," he says softly, "and I won't be able to keep my hands to myself."

"Yes, you will." I unlock the door and walk inside, willing my hormones to calm the hell down. "This home sits on about two acres and only has partial views of the water."

I describe the pros and cons of the building and then step through the sliding glass doors to breathe in the salty sea air as Hunter has a look around.

Get yourself together, Maeve.

He's just a man.

He'll buy a house, come here once or twice a year, and I'll likely hardly ever see him again. I mean, sure, I can flirt with him, but there's no need to behave like a randy teenager.

"That view is a no-go," he says as he joins me on the deck. "It's nice, but for the price, I want more water view."

"I understand. Well, we have an appointment to see the one you pointed out to me tomorrow. And I can show you others, as well. There are plenty of options."

His gaze falls to my mouth. "I'll see anything that you want to show me."

I lick my lips. "I'm sure we'll find you the perfect home."

His lips twitch. "The house. Right."

I laugh and shake my head. "Come on. Let's get out of here."

He helps me lock up the house once more, and when we're outside, I hold out my hand for him to shake. It seems silly, but I'm not exactly ready to jump in his arms and kiss him silly.

I don't want the man to take out a restraining order or anything.

"See you tomorrow," I say politely.

His hand is warm and firm in mine. Those eyes hold humor and interest. "See you."

"WHY DIDN'T YOU TELL ME?" I demand and unload clean glasses from the dishwasher behind the bar. Keegan's stocking liquor and making googly eyes at Izzy, his very pregnant wife. Not that I blame him. She's beautiful and simply glows with her pregnancy.

"Tell you what?"

"That we had a famous person in the pub yesterday. One who, by the way, I flirted with all night last night and ended up being my client today. If you'd have told me last night, I wouldn't have been blindsided today. Hell, I probably wouldn't have flirted with him so much either."

"Jesus, Maeve, I can't be responsible for giving you the lowdown on every single bleeding customer who walks through my doors, can I?"

"Famous ones, yes." I set the last clean glass on the shelf and get to work washing the dirty ones. "You could have said: *'By the way, that man down the bar is a famous fighter.'*"

"That's just ridiculous."

I turn to Izzy for backup. "Tell him it's not ridiculous."

"I'm not getting in the middle of this. Oh, and look at that, it's time for my nap." She kisses Keegan, waves at me, and escapes up the back stairs to the apartment above.

"How's she feeling?" I ask my brother.

"Ready to have a wee babe," he says with a proud smile. "And I'm ready right with her. It feels like this pregnancy has taken forever."

"You haven't even *known* her a year." I laugh and wipe down the bar. "Crazy to think about, isn't it? A year ago, you didn't even know her. And now, you're married and about to have a baby. Things can change so fast."

"For the better," he adds. "Because I wasn't truly alive until she walked through that door."

I stop and stare at him, feeling my heart shifting in my chest. "That might be the sweetest thing I've ever heard."

"We O'Callaghan men are a sappy bunch," he says with that Irish brogue and winks at me.

"I have to go check on my customers."

We haven't been open for the dinner crowd long, so only a few of my tables are full right now. In a couple of hours, we'll have a waiting line out the door, and I'll be busting my ass to keep up.

I check in with my tables, refill water, take fresh drink orders, and when I return to the bar, I stop short.

Sitting right there, at the end of the counter, is Hunter.

His eyes meet mine. They're full of humor and heat, and my freaking nipples tighten.

By the way his eyes fall to breast level and darken before returning to mine, I'd say he noticed.

"I need a pint of Guinness, a Coke, and two shots of whiskey," I say to Keegan as I set my tray on the bar for him to fill. "Hello, Mr. Meyers."

"Hunter," he says and reaches over to tuck a loose piece of my hair behind my ear. My entire body comes alive when he touches me. "You look beautiful this evening, Maeve."

I smirk, but his words make me want to preen.

I'm in my usual uniform of an O'Callaghan's Pub T-shirt, denim shorts, and sneakers. I tied up my hair and even scrubbed my face free of makeup because it just makes me feel grimy while I'm working.

But I'll take the compliment all the same.

"Can I put in a food order for you?" I ask him.

"What do you suggest?"

"Like I said last night, my mother's stew is wonderful. The best on the continent."

He blinks in surprise. "Then I guess I'd better try it."

"I'll go fetch it for you."

I swing through the doors leading to the kitchen and have to stop to catch my breath.

"Why do you look like that?" Shawn asks.

"Like what?" I do my best to keep my face bland, blinking innocently.

He waves his hand in my direction. "Like you're…"

"Turned on," Lexi finishes for him and grins at me.

"I don't know what you're talking about." I try to act nonchalant as I place the order for the stew. "I'll be right back for that."

I swing back through the doors, hurry into the restroom, and lean on the counter to catch my breath.

"Get it together, Maeve."

CHAPTER 3

"You're two different people."

I turn and frown at Hunter as I unlock the door of the house we've come to see.

My house.

"What do you mean? Are you saying I'm crazy?"

"No." He chuckles and closes the door behind him after we step inside. "It's interesting to see you in both of the places you work. They're so different. *You're* so different in them."

No one has ever noticed that before. It's not like my family hangs out with me while I sell houses. I have to turn my back to him and take a deep breath. It would help keep my libido in check if he didn't smell so damn good.

"I would think that the real estate market would be good enough here for you not to need the second job," he continues.

That has me turning back to him. "I *don't* need it. Working at the pub has always been a family thing. Shawn and Lexi are famous writers, but they still man the kitchen. We don't do it because we have to, but because we love it. I enjoy my family, Mr. Meyers."

"Hunter." He steps closer to me and reaches out to brush my hair over one ear.

"The truth is, there's more than enough real estate business to go around. The island is popular and expensive. And, given that it's not getting any bigger, there's only so much of it to go around. I've seen it change dramatically since I was younger."

"Does that bother you?" he asks.

"It used to." I shrug, prop my hands on my hips, and turn to look out the killer windows that have an incredible view of the ocean. "But then I realized that I could be miserable here, hate the change and the new people moving in, or I could embrace it, love it, culti-vate it."

"And now you sell homes here."

"I do. I love my island. I was so young when we moved here, it's really all I know. Okay, enough about me. You should wander through and have a look."

Please hate it. Please, please, please hate it.

"Why don't you show it to me?" he counters and holds his hand out for mine.

"Sure, if you'd rather. I just like to give prospective buyers a chance to look at their own pace." I find myself with my hand in his as we wander through the house. "Well, as you can see, the view is okay."

"Yeah, it's okay." He shakes his head. "It's fucking brilliant."

I shrug, not wanting to tell him how much I agree. "If you like that sort of thing."

I turn and gesture to the kitchen and living space.

"The owners updated the kitchen just a couple of years ago, so you have your pot filler above the stove, a deep farmhouse sink, and all of the bells and whistles, including a built-in coffee maker."

My dream coffee maker.

"The house is only about four-thousand square feet, so it's smaller than some of the others you've seen."

"I don't need anything huge," he says as he follows me up the stairs, and I hear him inhale sharply when we get to the top. "I like this space."

I glance around at the second living space. The staging company has it set up with a pool table, a wet bar, and a gaming place for the kids.

I would clear all of this out and make it a fabulous reading and relaxing space.

"There are three bedrooms on this level, including the master. The master suite is situated on the entire left side of the house."

I guide him through French doors that lead into the master bedroom, and step to the glass doors that open to the balcony beyond.

"Wow," he says as he steps outside with me and stares at the waves crashing below. "This is incredible."

"The waves are a little loud," I point out.

"I would keep the doors open and fall asleep to the sound of it."

So would I.

"It would get awfully cold in there." I gesture with my thumb to the bedroom.

"I'll just get a heated mattress pad and a nice, thick blanket, and it'll be fine."

I ignore that comment because that's precisely what I would do. Instead, I walk back inside to show him the rest.

"There are two separate master closets," I inform him. "A his and hers, so to speak, which I think is odd."

Or, you know, absolutely amazing.

"I think it's nice," he says, checking them out. "I have a lot of gear that I don't want mixing with other things, so it would work well."

Well, crap.

I follow him into the master bath and wait as he looks at the walk-in shower and the amazing tub with a view of the water behind it.

My heart sings when I walk through this house. This bathroom is *everything.* But I don't want him to think that.

"The tub is kind of small," I point out. "You're a big guy. You'd need more room."

He eyes the tub dubiously. It sits in the corner of the room with wide windows that look out to the water.

I've daydreamed about the bubble baths I'd take in this room.

"I think it looks plenty big."

I climb inside and sit. "See? It's barely big enough for *me*. And you're much bigger than I am."

He taps his finger to his lips, and then, to my utter shock, he just climbs right in with me.

"We *both* fit."

I stare at him, blinking. "It's a little tight in here."

Before I can get out, Hunter tugs me into his lap and cups my face. "What is it about you?" He murmurs, his eyes on my lips.

I can't help but lean into him. God, he just *feels* so good.

"This is kind of inappropriate," I whisper. I don't sound convincing even to my ears.

"Why?"

"Because you're my client."

He sighs and watches his thumb as it makes circles on the apple of my cheek.

"You know, I can respect that you're trying to be professional," he says softly. "I get that. But we're both adults here, Maeve."

He lifts his eyebrow, and I nod in agreement. "True. We are."

"And it's not like I'll be your client forever. Just until I find my house."

I can't help but nod. He's not wrong. I don't have to worry about a long-term working relationship with this man.

"That's true, too."

He leans in and kisses my forehead. Not my lips, like I expected. No, he kisses my *forehead.* And somehow, that's almost more intimate than the meeting of lips.

I swallow. Hunter takes a deep breath.

"Should we continue the tour?" I ask.

"Good idea." He lifts me off of his lap and helps me out of the tub. "Where are the other bedrooms?"

"There are two on the other side of the house, and there's a mother-in-law apartment above the garage."

"Rachel will love that," he mutters.

Rachel? Who's Rachel?

He'd asked *me* if I was taken yesterday, and we've flirted like it's our job. Hell, just thirty seconds ago in the tub, I would have sworn we'd had a special moment when all this time he's had a woman in his life named Rachel?

Why are men so horrible?

But I don't say anything as I follow him, staying quiet as he checks out the rest of the house.

"Let's have a look at the garage," he suggests.

"Sure." We walk downstairs and out the back door, under a short breezeway that leads to the garage. "There are three bays for vehicles in here. There's also an extra two acres of raw land for sale next door in case you want extra space for something like a shop."

"Or a gym." He nods and walks through the garage. "I like the built-ins. Let's go upstairs."

"The entrance is on the outside of the building." I lead him around the perimeter of the garage to the staircase on the backside. "There's a one-bedroom apartment up here, complete with a kitchenette."

And it would be absolutely perfect for my office space.

Or a guest house for my parents when they're here from Ireland.

He just nods and follows me back outside, then waits for me to lock the apartment before joining me in the kitchen.

"Listen, I have to get back to the city this afternoon," he says and tucks his thumbs into the pockets of his jeans, rocking back on his heels. "I have to get Rachel from my parents' place. But I'd like to come back on Thursday afternoon to keep looking. Do you think any of these places will sell in the next few days?"

"That's hard to say." I wish I could come up with the twenty-five grand I need for the down payment on this place. "I can tell you that the homes in this price range don't move quite as quickly."

"Good. I just need a couple of more days here before I decide."

"I can set up showings for Thursday afternoon, and anytime on Friday," I offer, elated that he didn't automatically buy *this* house. It's by far the best of all of the properties I've shown him.

His phone buzzes, he checks it, and then scowls. "I'll kill her."

"Do you often think about murdering your wife?"

He blinks up at me, that scowl still on his face. "Huh?"

"Never mind."

"I'm not married."

"Girlfriend, then."

"Rachel is my daughter." Worry and anger still line his face. "And she's testing my damn patience."

His daughter.

This sexy, cocky, arrogant yet endearing man is a father.

He's distracted as he takes one more look around the house and then starts walking toward the front door.

"I have to get back. But I'll see you on Thursday."

"Sure, okay." He's leaving. Why does that make me sad? I barely know this man. But I like him. I like him *a lot.*

He opens the door, pauses, and then hurries back to me, his face full of determination.

He cups my face, tugs the lip I didn't know I was biting out of my teeth, and swoops down to kiss me.

It's the kind of kiss that reaches down and makes a girl's knees weak.

He's surprisingly gentle but in control.

Determined.

And when he pulls back, he presses those talented lips to my forehead once more.

"Have a good week, Mr. Meyers."

"Hunter." He tips my chin up and grins down at me. "My name is Hunter, Maeve." He winks and then walks away again.

"Thursday," he tosses over his shoulder, and then the door closes behind him.

"Whoa." I press my fingertips to my lips and lean on the kitchen counter. "Holy hell, the man can kiss."

I make my way through the house, turning off lights and making sure the doors and windows are locked.

I *love* this home. I have since it was built about ten years ago. I've daydreamed about it.

And then, last Christmas, I was invited to a cookie exchange here with some friends and got to tour the inside.

It's everything I always dreamed of and more. That view off the back of the property is what every fiction writer thinks of when crafting a story full of intrigue and mystery.

There should be ghosts walking these cliffs.

Perhaps that's just my Irish roots talking.

"You have other things to do today," I remind myself. There's no time for dillydallying in someone else's house.

The truth is, I could ask my oldest brother, Kane,

for a loan for what I need to buy this house, and he'd give it to me in a heartbeat.

But I don't think it's right to ask for help with this sort of thing. I'll earn it. And, chances are, the house won't sell before I'm ready to buy anyway.

I close and lock the front door, climb into my car, and take off toward my house. I have just enough time to have a snack before my showing this afternoon.

I have no time for thinking about a man named Hunter, who makes me think about all kinds of sexy things.

"YOU NEED MORE CREAMER," Maggie, my only sister, says as she rinses the carton and tosses it into the recycling bin. "You've been really moody this week."

"I have not." I frown at her as she brings her cup of coffee to the table and sits with me. She arrived on my doorstep this morning with fresh cinnamon rolls.

Because Maggie and I often work evenings at the pub, breakfasts are our best time to catch up.

"You're not usually moody," she continues. "So something must be up. What's going on? Does it have anything to do with the hot boxer that came into the pub and made googly eyes at you?"

"First of all, he's not a boxer. He's a former MMA fighter. Second of all, he didn't make googly eyes at me."

Except, he totally did.

"You weren't watching from where I was," she says. "Trust me. His eyes were googly."

I won't even mention that his mouth was warm and soft on mine. Maggie would take that information and run with it in directions I'm not even willing to entertain.

"Are we going to the cemetery today?"

My sister scowls. "Why in the hell would we do that?"

"Oh, I don't know, maybe because this is the second anniversary of your husband's death. I mean, shouldn't we take flowers or something?"

"Are you drunk?" She scoffs and takes a bite of her breakfast. "Hell, no. He was a lying, cheating piece of shit. The only reason I'd go to his grave is to spit on it."

"But you're not bitter or anything." I laugh as she glares at me. "Okay, I get it. I just didn't know how you'd handle it."

"With coffee and sugar. And with you." She shrugs a shoulder. "I've moved on from all of that, thank God."

"With Cameron?" I feel my lips twitch, but then her eyes fill with tears, and I suddenly feel like a complete jerk. "Whoa, what happened with Cameron?"

"Nothing." She wipes a tear. "It's so dumb. And you keep changing the subject, which is really annoying. Tell me about the hot fighter."

"I don't know much about him," I insist. "He's from Seattle, has a kid, drives the most expensive car I've ever seen in person in my life, and kisses like the devil."

"Wait. Back it up. You kissed him?"

"I wasn't going to tell you that part, but you cried, and I needed to give you something to cheer you up."

"You *kissed* him."

"Actually, he kissed me. It was nice."

"How nice?"

I frown.

"Was it nice enough to do it again?"

"He's a client—"

"Oh, please." Maggie rolls her eyes. "Don't pull that on me. We all know you're professional and blah blah blah. But are you going to do the hot guy?"

"You're so romantic."

She just watches me, waiting for an answer.

"He hasn't asked me to *do him*."

Still, Maggie watches without her face changing.

"He's so…"—I wave my hand in the air—"cocky. I don't know what to do with that."

"You have three brothers, all of whom are cocky."

"Not like this."

My phone pings at my elbow, and I look down to see a text from Hunter.

Hunter: *I found some other houses I'd like to see this weekend. I'm sending links.*

Me: *Sounds good.*

"Is he flirting with you?"

"No, he's just telling me that he found some other houses to look at."

But my phone pings with another message.

Hunter: *Let's have lunch before we start on Thursday.*

I grin but reply with: *I can't.*

I set the phone aside and stare at my sister, who's just watching me with smug green eyes.

"What?"

"You'd totally do him."

My phone pings once more, and when I open the message, it's a selfie of Hunter, pouting. Then another text comes through.

Hunter: *Please?*

I laugh and reply.

Me: *Pouting doesn't work on me. But I guess I can shift my calendar. You're buying.*

"Okay, let's be honest here," Maggie says. "You like him. You should see the dumb look on your face right now."

"You're so sweet, Mary Margaret."

"I think it's nice," she insists. "But be careful with this one because he's super famous and probably has a legion of girls he's left behind."

"He has a *kid.*"

She nods. "Yeah, I Googled him. Read the Wiki. She's only fifteen. I mean, do you want to be a stepmom?"

"He's literally only a client right now," I remind us both. "No one has said a word about sex or being a damn stepmom. I *might* sell him a house, that's it. End of discussion."

"Except you kissed him."

"Do I have to marry every man who kisses me? Because if so, I'd have to marry Clifford Buckley from the eighth grade."

"And that would be unfortunate because poor Cliff doesn't look so hot these days."

"So, he has a fifteen-year-old daughter," I murmur and sip my coffee. "I wonder what the story is there."

Maggie looks like she's about to spew a bunch of information, but I hold up my hand, stopping her.

"No. It's none of my business. And if it ever becomes my business, I want to hear it from him. Okay?"

"Okay." She props her chin on her hand. "When's he coming back?"

"This week. I don't even know if he'll buy something. Maybe he's just one of those lookie-loos who want to see everything but then decides to go elsewhere."

"That would be annoying."

"Happens more than you think."

I sigh, and my phone pings again.

Hunter: *I managed to get away tomorrow afternoon rather than Thursday. Does that work for you?*

I grin. Today's Tuesday. It's only a day early if he comes tomorrow.

But I'm excited to see him again.

Still, I don't want to seem too eager.

Me: *I can shuffle some things around for you.*

I watch the three dots dance on my screen.

Hunter: *I'll see you tomorrow. Dinner?*

Me: *I really can't. And don't pout. I have to work.*

There's no reply, and I can't help but grin when I set my phone aside.

"I don't think I've ever seen you like this," Maggie says, catching my attention.

"Like what?"

"With little hearts bursting above your head. You're not usually one to crush on someone."

"Maybe I just don't tell you about it when I do."

She narrows her eyes at me. "No, you'd tell me. I hope this guy doesn't turn out to be a jerk and a half."

"Maybe just three-quarters of a jerk."

Maggie smirks. "That would be less than most guys."

"You know, Cameron's always been a nice guy, Mags. What in the world did he do to you now?"

"It's not that he *did* anything," she admits. "He's not a bad guy."

"Then why are you miserable?"

"Because he's done nothing at all," she repeats. "And it's damn annoying."

"Maybe you need to light a fire under his ass."

She doesn't say anything for a long minute and then shrugs one shoulder. "You know, just once, I'd like to be the priority without asking to be. I want him to *choose me.* Not because I ask him to but because he wants to. I want to feel important."

"Yeah, but he's not a mind reader."

"And that's the worst part. Because if he doesn't just instinctively want to be with me, to make me the number-one spot in his life, then there's no room for me at all. I'll never be with someone who loves everything else in his life more than me again. I can't do it, Maeve."

"No." I reach over and link my fingers with hers. "No, you can't. You're right. When was the last time you spoke with him?"

"It's been a few weeks." She shrugs as if it's no big deal.

But I know it is.

"I might go on a date with someone else."

I blink quickly, surprised. "Who?"

"I don't know yet. I have to figure that part out."

"Good for you." I squeeze her hand and then let go. "Go get them."

CHAPTER 4

I've spent the better part of the last two days with her. She's shown me six more homes, including the one we're in now, and last night, I spent several hours at the pub where I nursed one beer, ate my weight in that amazing stew, and took it all in.

Took *her* in. I can't get enough of the way Maeve laughs, of the way she moves. Hell, I was only away from her for a couple of days and I *missed* her.

Not to mention, I like what I've seen of Maeve's family business.

I'm close to my parents and am grateful to have them close by. But I'm an only child, so watching the O'Callaghans and the way they interact, how they work together, has been an education.

"I didn't realize until he came into the pub last night that Kane O'Callaghan is your brother," I say as I glance at another kitchen. "I have a few pieces of his glass in my home. Bought them at a charity thing a few years ago."

She grins in that proud way she does when she thinks of her family. Her smile lights up any room. Yeah, it's cliché, and no, I don't give a rat's ass.

"That's awesome," she says. "Yeah, Kane's the only one of us who doesn't put some time in at the pub. But he's always in his glass barn, making something new, or traveling, or just enjoying his wife and their son. The pub was never for him, and that's okay. He comes in from time to time to look in on us all."

"And your parents?"

"They're in Ireland right now," she says. "But are headed this way in a few days because Izzy's about to have that baby any moment, and they wouldn't miss that for the world."

"You're a tight family."

She nods slowly. "When we came here from Ireland, we were all each other had. It was us against the rest of the world, so to speak. It helped that we all speak English. But, of course, with thick accents, we were still outsiders."

"You don't have much of an accent," I point out, itching to touch her. To pull her to me. To kiss the hell out of her.

I simply brush her thick, soft hair behind her shoulder.

"No, I was pretty young when we moved here. Kane and Keegan have the strongest accents. Mine comes and goes—if I'm angry, especially. Sometimes, I turn it up at the pub just for fun."

I smile and watch her walk to the windows that look out at the ocean. She does that in every house we see. Stands by the windows or on a balcony, staring out at the water like she's drawn to it.

"Do you live on the waterfront?" I ask, wanting to know more about her.

"No." That's it. No explanation. And before I can ask, she turns to me and props her hands on her hips. "Okay, Hunter, this is it. The very last house for sale on this island that has a water view, is move-in ready, and fits most of what you asked for."

"We've seen a lot this past week," I agree with a nod. But it's not enough, because this means that I can't use it as an excuse to see her anymore.

"I'm going to be blunt."

"By all means."

"Are you actually going to buy something? Or are you a lookie-loo just wasting my time?"

"A lookie-loo?"

"You know…" She sighs and rubs her fingers on her forehead in either frustration or fatigue. Either way, I don't like it. And the thought of her stress being because of me makes me even less happy about it. "Someone who wants to see everything but has no interest in actually buying. Because that's just a waste of my time—and yours. Both of our time is valuable."

"I'm not a lookie-loo." I shove my hands into my

pockets so I don't reach out for her, hug her to me, and try to calm the nerves I see humming just beneath the surface. I keep my distance. Because although she's been nothing but *nice* since I got here, we haven't been flirting the way we were a couple of days ago.

And it's damn frustrating.

"I knew the second we walked into that house on Sunday, the one I showed you on my phone the day before, that it was the one I want."

"Then, why—?"

"I wanted to keep seeing you," I continue, interrupting her. "You won't let me take you out for dinner, so I kept looking at houses with you. I just wanted to be with you."

Her mouth opens as if she wants to say something, but she closes it again.

"I'm not in the habit of being interested enough in someone to make this kind of effort, if we're being completely honest. Not in a *very* long time, anyway."

She frowns. "You've been looking at houses just to hang out with me?"

"Yeah." I swallow. "When you put it like that, it sounds a little desperate. Don't call the press with that info, okay?"

She takes a deep breath, lets it out, and then chuckles. "Well, I guess I'll get the paperwork started on the other place. Do you know how much you want to offer?"

"What's the price of it again?"

She tells me, and I nod, thinking it over. "Let's add fifty thousand to the asking price and seal the deal. If I can take ownership in the next couple of weeks, that would be even better."

She blinks, pulls her phone out of her purse, and makes some notes. "I'll see what I can do, Mr. Meyers."

I tip my head to the side, watching her. "Hunter. My name is Hunter."

"Of course. Shall we go, then? I'll get the papers ready for you to sign this afternoon, and I'll start making some calls."

I don't know where the sudden cold shoulder is coming from, but I don't like it. "What's wrong?"

"What? Oh, nothing. I just want to get this all wrapped up for you."

"No, something's wrong. You just went cold on me."

She shakes her head and tries to look innocent.

It doesn't work.

"Maeve."

"You should have just told me on Sunday that you wanted m—*the* house. Your offer likely would have been accepted by now."

"I told you, I wanted to see you."

"You're playing a game." Her voice is harder now. Jesus, are those *tears* in her eyes? "I don't have time for games. I'm a busy woman with responsibilities, and while it's flattering that you wanted to see me, it's just…not fair."

"Not fair?"

"No. Not fair. Anyway, I'll get paperwork drawn up for your signature and put the offer in. I'll have it ready for you in a couple of hours."

"Maeve," I say after she starts stalking to the front door, her heels clicking on the hardwood. "Wait."

"Like I said, I'm busy."

"Damn it, Maeve O'Callaghan, wait just a goddamn minute." I catch up to her and tug on her arm, mortified that there *are* tears in her eyes. "Honey, what's wrong?"

"Don't call me *honey.*" She swipes angrily at the tears and shakes her head. "Nothing. I'm fine."

"You're not fine."

"I'm *fine.* I just need to be alone, that's all. I have to go."

"Maeve." I can't stand it. I turn her to me, pull her against me, and bury my lips in her hair, holding her gently. "Talk to me. If you don't tell me what I did wrong, I can't fix it."

She clings to me for a moment, her hands fisting in my shirt near my waist. Her forehead rests on my chest.

But rather than lean into me, she pulls back.

"There's nothing to fix. I'm being stupid, and I apologize for being emotional."

"Do you really hate the house that much? I know you tried to talk me out of it when we were there, but—"

"It's the most beautiful house I've ever seen in my

life," she interrupts, and her bottom lip wobbles. "I don't hate it at all. I must just have something in my eye. It's ridiculous."

"Stop." My voice is firm because this is one area I won't ever budge on. "No lying, Maeve. It's my number-one rule."

"I really *don't* hate it."

"And you really don't have anything in your eye."

"I was going to buy it, okay?" she whispers, shocking the hell out of me. "The house. I've been saving up for it. But I'm still too far away from the down payment. It's just not meant to be, and I know you and your daughter will be happy there."

"Well, hell." I shove my hands through my hair and feel like the biggest prick on earth. "Jesus, Maeve, I'll give you the money to buy it."

She stares at me, shocked. "Don't be ridiculous."

"You're miserable. I feel like I just kicked a puppy."

Her spine straightens, all evidence of tears dries from her eyes, and she firms that gorgeous little chin.

"I'm no puppy. I'm perfectly fine, and it's a beautiful home for you and your daughter. I'll have the papers for you later today."

She turns to leave, and before I can reach out to take her hand and keep her with me just a moment longer, she turns back to me.

"Are you still interested in dinner?"

My eyebrows climb in surprise. "Hell, yes. Don't play with my emotions here, Maeve."

A smile touches the edges of her lips. "I don't have to work at the pub tonight."

"Well, then, I'll pick you up at six."

She nods. "Okay. I'll be ready. I'll text you my address."

"I CAN'T BELIEVE you brought me all the way over to Seattle just for dinner," she says and takes a bite of her steak.

"There's a method to my madness," I admit as I watch her chew.

Jesus, Mary, and Joseph, she has the sexiest fucking lips I've ever seen. And she tastes like heaven.

"And what is that?" she asks.

"I get to be with you during the travel time, as well as dinner."

She laughs and lifts her martini, those green eyes shining at me over the rim as she takes a sip.

"We talked about my family earlier today," she says. "Tell me about *your* family."

"There's not much to tell. My parents live here in the Seattle area, and I see them often. And I have Rachel."

"How long have you been divorced?"

"I was never married." I narrow my eyes on her. "Don't you already know all of this?"

"How would I?"

"I don't know, Google?"

She shakes her head. "No. I avoid Google. I have several members of the family who are famous, and I know that the truth isn't always portrayed online. I'd much rather get to know you from *you* directly. If you want to tell me about yourself, you will."

"Besides Kane, who else is famous in your family?"

She grins. "Well, because Kane married Anastasia, we have Luke Williams, Leo Nash, and Will Montgomery. Not to mention Starla, the pop star, and Amelia Montgomery, the YouTube sensation who has a makeup line. It's awesome, by the way. There may be more, but those are off the top of my head. Also, if I didn't again mention Shawn and his wife, my brother would kill me."

"Wait, you know Jules McKenna's family?"

She tilts her head to the side. "Yes, they're extended family now. Do *you* know them?"

"Hell, I practically grew up with Nate. He's a bit older than me, but I pretty much lived in his dad's gym as a teenager. Yeah, I know them well."

"What a small world," she says with a smile.

"That's a lot of famous people," I reply, thinking it over. "Holy shit, Maeve."

"I know." She finishes her steak and reaches for her martini glass again. "Trust me, it gets intimidating. And, sometimes, we need graphs and charts. Oh! And Izzy, Keegan's wife, is a local celebrity. She reports the weather here in Seattle."

"*That's* where I know her from," I say, thumping my fist on the table. "It's been driving me nuts."

Maeve laughs and nods. "Yep. She doesn't have to work at the pub, but she enjoys it, so she helps out a couple of days a week. But now we're just talking about *my* family again."

"Right." I smile and take a sip of my water. "I was a young fighter and met this woman, Carla. She was nineteen and what we call a ring bunny."

Maeve laughs. "Of course, you do. That's not sexist at all."

"Oh, it totally is. I was twenty. What the fuck did I know? Anyway, Carla was cute and paid me a lot of attention. We hooked up a few times, and the next thing I knew, she was pregnant. By that time, she'd moved on to a different fighter, a guy named Danny Ost. He's still in the business. Anyway, she made it clear that she had no interest in a kid."

Maeve's eyes widen.

"At first, she talked about aborting it. And it's not that I don't believe in a woman's right to choose, but I sat her down and told her that if she'd carry it, I would be responsible for it. Carla didn't come from a stable home. She would have had *zero* help. And, yeah, I could have taken the easy way out, but something in my gut said: *Do this.*

"So, what felt like the blink of an eye later, I had this tiny pink thing to take care of. I wasn't willing to stop fighting—and thank God for my parents. Seriously, they're saints. I bought them a house and retired them both early. If I could do more, I would. Because they brought Rachel into their lives, and they love her as much as I do."

"Of course. My family would do the same."

"I can see that," I agree.

"Does Rachel ever see her mother?"

"Carla comes and goes. She's a free spirit, but she checks in with Rach now and then. Rachel just can't depend on Carla to show up when she says she will. And last year, she embarrassed Rachel at school. She showed up out of the blue and sat down at the lunch table with her. So, Rachel's figuring out what kind of person her mom is."

"You're a good dad," Maeve says. "A lot of people would talk a lot of crap about a parent like that."

"Hey, she did what I asked. She had the baby. That's all I ever wanted from her." I scribble my name on the credit card receipt. "So, that's about it for my family."

My phone rings, and I glance down to see Rachel's name.

"This is Rachel. I have to take it. Hello?"

"Dad, I need you to come get me."

I narrow my eyes. "From Gram and Gramps'?"

"No." Her voice is thin. "I snuck out. But I—"

"I'm tracing your phone right now. I'll be there in just a few minutes. Are you safe?"

"Yeah, I guess."

"Don't move. I'm on my way."

I click off and swear under my breath.

"Is she okay?"

"I don't know what the hell is going on, but I have to go get her. I'm sorry."

"What for? She's your *daughter*. Let's go."

We hurry through the restaurant and out to my car so I can check my phone to see where my daughter is.

"She's on my last damn nerve."

"You said that before. Has she been in trouble?"

"Yeah. That's why we're moving to the island. She's *always* in trouble lately. Her friends are awful. She's defiant. And she's started to give my parents a hard time. She just admitted to me that she snuck out of their house tonight."

I feel my jaw clench in anger.

"Speaking of, I'd better call them."

I make the call on Bluetooth in the car, and my dad answers.

"How are things going on the island?" he asks in greeting.

"They've gone well, but I'm in Seattle. I came into the city to have dinner with Maeve."

"Oh, the woman you told me about?"

I feel Maeve whip her head to stare at me. "Yes, that's the one. Listen, I just got a call from Rachel. She snuck out and needs me to come get her. I'm on my way."

"Damn it," Dad mutters. "Hunter, I swear to you, we've been on that girl like white on rice all damn day."

"She's sneaky. And I'm over it. When I'm done with her, she'll think being a nun is liberating. I'll keep you posted."

"Please do."

I click off as we approach a gas station, the exact location of the red dot on my phone.

"What's she doing here?" I mutter as I pull in and see my daughter standing by the front doors, waiting.

"Uh, should I get in the back?" Maeve asks, dubiously eyeing the minuscule backseat. The Rolls is a little sportster, not really meant for hauling around more than two people.

"No." I pull to a stop and climb out of the car to address my daughter. "You'll have to climb into the backseat."

"Who's that?" Rachel demands.

"My friend." Jesus, I've never introduced my daughter to a woman I've dated before. As far as she knows, I'm an eternal bachelor. "Backseat."

I hold my seat forward for her to slip behind. Once she's squeezed into the back, I reenter the car and pull out of the gas station parking lot.

"Who are you?" Rachel asks.

"I'm Maeve," the woman next to me says. "Nice to meet you."

Before Rachel can say *anything* else, I give her a hard look in the rearview mirror. "Talk to me."

"I just decided I didn't want to go do what my friends wanted to do."

"Why in the ever-loving hell were you out in the first place? You know you're supposed to be at Gram and Gramps' while I'm out of town."

"Well, apparently, you *aren't* out of town. You're just having a sex weekend with this...*person.*"

"Watch it," I warn her. "Why did you leave the house?"

"Because I wanted to go hang with my friends."

"That's not a good reason."

I pull through the gate to my house and drive up the steep driveway toward the garage.

"Why are we at home?" Rachel asks. "Aren't we going to Grams'?"

"No." I pull up to the house and get out of the car, holding the seat for Rachel. As soon as she's standing next to me, I smell her breath. "You've been drinking."

"I had *one* beer."

"You're fifteen fucking years old," I remind her, my voice like steel. "You're not an adult."

"You treat me like a *baby,*" she counters. "I called you because they were snorting coke, and I didn't want to do that stuff."

"*Coke?*" I stare at her in disbelief. "Jesus Christ, Rachel. You're done with them. You've just lost your phone and every other privilege you enjoy."

"Dad—"

"Wait." We both turn at the sound of Maeve's voice. My chest is heaving, my blood rushing through my ears. "She just told you what happened. She called you for *help*. I know that what she did was wrong, but she also did the right thing by not doing the drugs and calling you instead. You can't punish her for her friends' decisions."

I narrow my eyes, but I know she's right.

"I like her," Rachel decides and turns to Maeve. "Not that you'll be around for long because no one ever is. But I like you."

My daughter tosses her phone to me and then stomps into the house, leaving me out in the driveway with Maeve.

"I'm sorry, I shouldn't have interrupted," she begins, but I shake my head.

"No, you were right. I was upset, and I can't punish her for what her friends decided to do. I'm glad she called me, but I'm so damn pissed that she snuck out in the first place."

"Absolutely." Maeve checks her watch. "I'd better hunt down a hotel room. I'd call an Uber to take me back to the island, but I think I've missed the last ferry for the day."

"Ah, hell. I'm so sorry. Why don't you stay here tonight? I'll take you home first thing in the morning."

She calmly looks back to the front door where Rachel just slammed it and shakes her head. "I think, under the current circumstances, that's not at all appropriate."

She looks back at me and raises a brow.

My heart skips a beat.

"Maeve."

"It's okay." She walks forward and takes my hand in hers, giving my fingers a little squeeze. "I'll grab a room."

"I'll pick you up in the morning and take you home."

"I'd like that." She smiles and then reaches up to cup my cheek. I feel my heart, the one that just skipped a beat, shift. "She's going to be okay. And so are you. I enjoyed tonight."

"I wish you'd stay with me."

Her smile is quick and full of female satisfaction. "Another night. When there isn't so much teenage angst going on."

"That could take five years."

She laughs and taps on the screen of her phone, then leans in to hug me.

"My car will be here in three minutes. I have to meet them down at the gate."

"I'll walk you down."

We start down the driveway. "Aren't you afraid she'll sneak out again?"

"Nah. This place is like Fort Knox. She's not going anywhere else tonight. But I might sneak out later and come find your hotel."

Maeve's laugh fills the air. "You'd best set a good example for your daughter."

"You're a bossy one, you know that?"

She leans her head on my biceps. I can't get enough of her touch. "Yeah. I am."

Her car pulls up to the gate. I watch her get into the backseat and then stare at the red taillights as the car pulls away.

I have to go up and have a long talk with my daughter.

CHAPTER 5

~MAEVE~

"What hotel?" Maggie asks with a frown as she stares at me on FaceTime.

"Uh, the Four Seasons," I reply with a chuckle. "I figured if I'm stuck in Seattle for the night, it might as well be at a really nice place."

"Fancy," she replies with a grin. "I'm sorry that happened, though."

"He has a teenager." I shrug and sip the wine I had brought up. "I just feel bad for *him*. Sounds like she's a handful."

"I think Ma and Da had it kind of easy with us. I don't remember any of us pulling stuff like that."

I purse my lips and then giggle. "You're too young to remember Kane stumbling into the house, drunk at sixteen, trying to act nonchalant. I thought Da was going to kill him. And then there was the time that Keegan got caught trying to have sex with Elizabeth

Scooner in his car in the park. The cops called Da on that one. Threatened to charge Keegan with indecent exposure."

Maggie's eyes go wide, and then she busts up laughing. "Okay, never mind. We should really buy them presents more often than just holidays."

"Flowers every single day," I agree with a nod. "Anyway, I just wanted to let you know that I won't be home until sometime tomorrow morning, but I should be at the pub for my evening shift."

"Just let me know if you can't make it, and we'll figure it out," Maggie replies with a yawn. "Oh, guess what?"

"What?"

"I have a date tomorrow. A morning date because I work nights."

"With who?" I sit up in surprise. "Mary Margaret, you have to tell me everything."

"This guy, Eddie, who works at the gym, asked me out. I thought, *what the hell?* So, while you're coming home tomorrow, I'll be eating waffles and staring at a hot musclehead guy."

"I want to know everything," I say and point at her. "Be safe. Call me when you're done."

"Yes, mother. Okay, I'd better get back out there. It's actually pretty quiet tonight, for a summer evening."

"Have a good night."

"You, too." She blows me a kiss and hangs up. I lean against the pillows of the bed. This place is *posh.* I wouldn't usually splurge like this, but now that I know I won't be buying my dream home, I figured I deserved something extra indulgent tonight.

I never realized that a person could mourn for a *thing*. But I sure had a bad moment this afternoon when I drafted those papers. The owners moved to Phoenix, so I suspect that Hunter will be able to take ownership quickly. The furniture inside is for staging. As soon as papers are signed, we'll have the company come and empty it out.

Realistically, it can all happen pretty quickly.

I'll find another house. There's always another one. Or, I'll buy a lot when one comes up for sale and build.

There are options.

In the meantime, I have a great home. It's not like I'm homeless or anything.

I sip my wine, and my phone suddenly rings at my elbow. I look down and smile.

"Hello there."

"Did you get to your hotel okay?" Hunter asks. His voice is soft in my ear. I can't help but wonder how it would sound if his lips were pressed directly to my skin, and a rush of pleasure moves through me.

"I did." I grin and sip my wine. "I'm in my room, wrapped in the robe they provide, with a glass of wine in hand. This turned into a little vacation."

"Well, that sounds a hell of a lot better than the icy silence in my house tonight."

"She's fifteen, Hunter," I remind him gently. "It's her civic duty to make your life difficult."

"She's good at it." There's a smile in his voice now. "I tried to talk to her, but she's just mad."

"Give her a day or two. She'll relax a bit."

"You sound so sure."

"I know it's easy for me to say, given that I don't have any kids, and she's not living with *me*. But I was a fifteen-year-old girl once. After a couple of days, I'd soften a bit." I sigh and turn onto my side. "You know, if you can't get away tomorrow, I'll call one of my brothers to come get me. It's really not a big deal."

"It's a big deal," he counters. "I'll be the one to take you home."

I grin, grateful that he insisted. I *want* to see him again. I don't know where this is going or what we're doing, but I'm enjoying him.

"Okay."

"What are you going to do with the rest of your evening?" he asks.

"Well, I don't usually sleep much. But, I don't have my computer with me, so I'm being forced to relax. Which means I'll likely find movies on TV and veg out. Maybe I'll order up some junk food, too."

"I'll be right over."

I laugh, enjoying him. "Maybe, someday, we can have a redo of tonight and veg out together."

"I suspect I'd have other things in mind to do with

you in that hotel room," he says. "And it wouldn't include being lazy."

"Oh? What *would* it include, Mr. Meyers?"

He sighs. "I'll be happy to show you. Sooner rather than later. Now, before I say a bunch of stuff that I might regret later, I'll let you go be lazy. I'm going to hit the punching bag for a while and get some of this pent-up energy out."

I grin. "Okay. I'll see you tomorrow. Just text me whenever you're ready. I'm at the Four Seasons."

"You have good taste, Maeve."

"Of course, I do. Good night."

"'Night."

"WHY DON'T you come inside and I'll make you break-fast?" I ask Hunter the next morning. He's just pulled up in front of my house, and it's only mid-morning. "I didn't eat anything this morning."

"No room service?"

"Just coffee," I admit. "Come on. I make a mean omelet."

We climb out of his car, and I walk ahead of him to my front door, unlock it, and then walk inside.

"I like your house," he says.

"I do, too. I'll give you a quick tour." I lead him up the stairs. "It's a small, historic home. Built in 1922, it's only twelve hundred square feet. Three bedrooms, two baths."

I give him some of the particulars and show him my favorite spots. My office. My reading space. And then we end up downstairs in my kitchen.

"The people who owned it before me did all the upgrades, which is awesome. I'm not a fan of construction. It's been a good home."

"But not your forever home," he says as I gather all of the ingredients for our breakfast from the fridge. He sits on a stool at the island and watches me. When he leans on his elbows and his arm muscles flex, I have to take a quick breath.

Good God, his muscles do things to me.

"No," I say and swallow hard. "I'd like to be on the water. It reminds me of Ireland."

"Really?"

"Yes. My family is from the west coast of Ireland, in a little village near Galway. So, I'm drawn to the sea. I just feel…at peace there. I'll end up there eventually. In the meantime, this house suits me."

I dice up some mushrooms, toss them into a bowl, and then reach for a red bell pepper.

"Oh, speaking of houses, let me check my email." I open the laptop sitting on the counter and tap some keys. Sure enough, there's an email waiting for me. "Just as I thought, they accepted your offer. Congratulations."

He smiles, but then the light leaves his eyes.

"What's wrong?"

"I feel like a dick for stealing the house out from under you."

"If it wasn't you, it would have been someone else. I promise." I shrug a shoulder. "Be happy about this. I'm happy for you. It's a great spot."

"You're so calm about it today."

"Yeah. I got over it." I crack some eggs into a bowl for whisking.

"How soon do you think we can move in?"

"Well, I have to call the current owners' realtor, but I suspect it could happen quickly." I explain to him about the couple already being gone. "We just need an inspection and the title company to push things through."

"Do you think I can move in sooner? Sort of rent it from them until the particulars are straightened out?"

"You really are in a hurry."

"I have several reasons for wanting to be here quickly." His eyes smolder as they fix on me, and I feel myself flush as I would have as a teenager.

"I think we can probably work something out."

"Great, I'll start calling movers today."

I heat a pan on the stove, drop the eggs in, and then work quickly to make the omelet perfect. When I slide it onto a plate and pass it to Hunter, he grins.

"You're gorgeous, *and* you cook?"

"A woman of many talents." I wink at him and get to

work on another omelet. My phone rings, and I quickly grab it to answer.

"Maggie? Are you okay?" I put the phone on speaker so Hunter can hear.

"He wasn't a serial killer," she replies. "But he's also not my soul mate."

"I mean, maybe your expectations are a little high," I suggest and toss some veggies in with my eggs. "You were going for soul mate on your first date?"

"It's a figure of speech. He's not for me. But that's okay, it was just breakfast. I didn't give him a blow job in the parking lot or anything."

Hunter sputters on his coffee, and I can't help but giggle.

"Wait, who's there?"

"I'm making breakfast for Hunter," I inform her. "I should have said you were on speaker."

"Well, at least I didn't say that I *did* give Eddie a blow job. That would have been more embarrassing. Okay, have fun. I'll talk to you later."

"Later."

I click off and grin over at Hunter. "Never a dull moment."

"I'd like to discuss this blow job in the parking lot option."

I bark out a laugh. "No way. I'm more of a blow job at home kind of girl."

His brown eyes narrow, but they're full of humor and fun. "That works, too."

"Eat your omelet."

~

I'm in a mood.

My hot water heater gave up the ghost this morning, so I had to take a cold shower. Added to that, my garbage disposal also decided to die on me after I'd already put half an onion down there. Now, my kitchen smells like a back alley.

Not to mention, I stubbed my toe after getting out of bed this morning.

And when I tried to get under the sink to check out the disposal, I banged my face on the cabinet when I tried to sit up too fast, and now I have a shiner.

Basically, I should just go back to bed, pull the covers over my head, and pray that this has all been a horrible dream.

But I can't. Because I'm an adult and have to do adult things.

It doesn't help that I haven't seen or heard from Hunter since he left here last week. Sure, I know he's been busy moving, but can't the man send a text? A freaking smoke signal?

"Probably just busy," I remind myself as I scroll through the listings on Google for a repairman. "Because the man has a *life.* And a kid. And he's moving. It's not like you're the center of the universe."

I blow out a breath through my lips just as my doorbell rings.

Did the repairman know to come through osmosis?

I don't even care that I look like crap. When I open the door, I'm suddenly swept up in the kiss of the century.

Hunter frames my face, and his magical lips tease and taunt mine until we're both breathless. Until my knees are weak, and I'm not entirely sure what year it is.

He pulls back and smiles down at me. "Hi."

"Hey." I swallow hard. "Were you just in the neighborhood?"

He chuckles. "Sort of. I haven't seen you all week."

"Haven't called me either."

He winces. "I'm sorry. I was busting ass to get Rachel here on the island, and by the time I'd finish for the night, I crashed. Moving is fucking exhausting. But we're here now."

His eyes narrow as he examines my face.

"Who the fuck put their hands on you?"

"Huh?" I frown, and he turns my face to the side, intent on my eye. "Oh, no one. I'm not a brawler. I hit my face on the cabinet. It hurts. I don't know how you tolerate taking shots to the face all the time."

"The goal is to knock *them* out before they get a shot in." His expression softens and he leans in to press his lips gently to the bruise. "I don't like seeing you marked up like that."

"I'll be okay," I assure him, tingling all over from his lips. "I'm glad you got moved in."

"I want to show you something." His grin is contagious.

I nod. "Okay."

"We have to go somewhere," he says and takes my hand, linking our fingers.

"Hunter, I can't go. First of all, I look like crap. Second of all, my house is falling apart."

His whole demeanor changes. He's all business now as he steps the rest of the way inside and shuts the door behind him.

"What's going on?"

"Don't worry, I'm about to start making some calls."

He turns back to me. "What's going on, Maeve?"

I sigh in defeat and give him a rundown of my morning. "I just need a couple of hours to get things handled here."

"I can have a look at the garbage disposal," he offers, but I shake my head no.

"Trust me, you do *not* want to go in there. I have a list of guys here to call."

"Let's do this. You go change and take a deep breath. I'll call these guys. I'll get this all taken care of."

I frown at him. "Why on earth would you do that?"

"Because I can. Now, go. I've got this."

He takes my phone to reference the numbers and starts tapping his screen. When I don't move, he raises his brows and makes a *shoo* motion with his hand.

"Yeah, I'm calling because I need someone to come look at a water heater."

I grin as I walk away and start up the stairs to my bedroom. When was the last time I had someone here to do something like that?

I can't remember. I might have been living at home with my parents.

It's not that I'm not *capable* of doing these things by myself. But, man, it's nice to let someone else handle it.

I quickly change into jeans and a tank top and am just sliding my feet into flip-flops when Hunter steps into my bedroom.

"A guy named Gil will be by at three this afternoon to have a look at all of it. He said the consult is free."

"Wow, okay. Thanks."

"No problem. Ready?"

"I think so. This is as good as it gets with this shiner."

"You look fantastic."

He leads me out to his car and drives us the mile or so to *his* new house.

"I want to show you what we've done," he admits with a grin before climbing out of the car and hurrying around to the passenger side to open the door for me. "Rachel actually *likes* it. I mean, she still has a bit of her attitude, but she smiled when she saw the house. She really wanted the apartment above the garage, which was a no-go. But I told her if she proved to me that I could trust her, it's a possibility down the line."

"Good idea." I follow him through the front door and smile when I take it all in. The furniture is modern but comfortable in earthy colors that match wonderfully with the trees and earth outside the wide windows. "Oh, I love this furniture."

"I was relieved that what I already had looked so good in here," he admits. "I was prepared to buy all new stuff, but when the movers set everything in place, it just clicked."

"It's great," I agree.

He leads me through the house, and I'm utterly charmed by the beautiful décor. It's not outrageous or in-your-face. The colors are earthy, the fabrics cozy.

It's a home that I'd feel comfortable curling up in.

"This is Rachel's room," he says and knocks on the closed door. When he hears the muffled, "*Come in*," he turns the knob, and we poke our heads in. "I brought Maeve to see how we're doing over here."

"Oh, hi." Rachel smiles shyly.

"This bedroom is beautiful," I say, meaning every word. "Your bed is gorgeous and totally suits a beach house."

"Yeah." She grins at the cream headboard that looks like half of a clamshell. "I just need help finding new curtains and stuff."

"Thank God you didn't bring all that black crap from the other house," Hunter says.

"I was going through a goth phase," she informs him and rolls her eyes.

"Well, I'm grateful that phase is over," Hunter replies with a wink.

"I could probably help you," I offer casually. "I have a good eye for that stuff."

"I don't want it to look like an old lady's room," Rachel warns me, making me laugh in surprise.

"I guess I won't show you any of my geriatric ideas, then." I laugh once more and glance around. "We can totally do this."

"Okay, I guess we can try. I don't even want to think about what Dad would pick." Rachel smiles. "Dad said you were pretty cool."

"Did he?" I glance at Hunter and then back at Rachel. "Well, I try. Do you like chicken wings and fries?"

"Sure, who doesn't?"

"Well, if you come into my family pub with your dad for dinner, the wings are on me. But no beer this time."

She winces. "I think I'm off of the beer for a *long* time."

"As it should be. You have time for those kinds of shenanigans. Don't try to grow up too fast. It happens fast enough as it is."

"I wish it would go faster." She sighs but then shrugs. "The pub sounds cool. Dad said the food is good."

I smile at Hunter. "It's the best on the island."

"Did you ask her?" Rachel asks Hunter, who shakes

his head, but his eyes are still full of humor.

"Ask me what?"

"Ask her, Dad," Rachel insists.

"Did I raise you to be bossy?"

Rachel just grins at him. She's a lovely young woman, with dark, straight hair and big brown eyes. She's slim and tall like her father.

"Is someone going to ask me something?"

Hunter nods. "I need to be in Los Angeles in two weekends, and I'd like for you to come with me."

"Well, I usually work at the pub on the weekends, but I can probably get someone to cover for me. What's in LA?"

"He's—"

"Hey, this is *my* story," he says, interrupting his daughter. She folds her lips in but is clearly bursting with anticipation.

"I'm a presenter at the ESPYs," he says. "And I'm nominated in a couple of categories."

I blink at him, look at Rachel, who's grinning widely, and then focus back on Hunter.

"What categories are you nominated in?"

"Fighter of the year, and athlete of the year."

I blink again in surprise. "Holy mackerel, Hunter, that's fantastic! Congratulations."

"Thanks. I don't usually take a date to these things—"

"More like has *never* taken a date," Rachel mutters, earning a pointed look from her father.

"But I'd really like it if you would join me."

"Is Rachel going, too?" I ask.

"Nah, I'm staying at Gram and Gramps'. And, yes, I *promise* to be a perfect child while you're gone so you don't have to worry about anything."

"So, what do you think? Wanna go hang out in LA for a day or two?"

"Well, sure." I press my lips together, suddenly panicking.

"What's wrong?"

"I have to find something to wear, and I only have two weeks to do it."

Hunter and Rachel both laugh.

"You'll find something awesome," Rachel says.

Is this the same child I saw just last week? Sure, she still rolls her eyes at her dad, but she's calmed down considerably.

"I'll make some calls," I reply. "Wow, thanks for inviting me."

"Thanks for saying yes."

CHAPTER 6

~HUNTER~

I want to drag her down the hall to my new bedroom, toss her onto the bed, and devour every fucking inch of her.

The way she's blushing just because I invited her to LA with me, and the kind way she interacts with my kid are both turn-ons.

Hell, I've been a walking hard-on since the night I saw her in her pub several weeks ago.

I can't get enough of her.

"Can we look at stuff for my room now?" Rachel asks Maeve and holds up her iPad. "There aren't a lot of places to shop on the island. Trust me, I checked."

"You're right," Maeve says. "Ordering will be best. I have time, if your dad doesn't care."

"Knock yourselves out," I reply and grin when Maeve sets her bag on top of Rachel's dresser and sits on the bed with my daughter.

"Did someone hit you?" Rachel asks her quietly.

"No," Maeve says with a laugh. "I'm just clumsy, and my sink sucks."

"Oh, good. Because if someone hit you, my dad might kill them."

I grin and back out of the bedroom, leaving them alone to shop online. My baby girl isn't wrong. If someone had put their hands on Maeve, they would regret it.

I go ahead and get back in the car, zoom over to Maeve's place, and walk through the unlocked front door and back to her kitchen with a small toolbox in hand.

It smells pretty ripe.

I flip the switch under the sink, but nothing happens.

It takes thirty minutes, some fiddling and cursing, but I finally get her disposal back in working order.

When I return to the new house and walk up to Rachel's room, I find the two pointing at something on the screen and giggling.

"Oh, man, Dad would *hate* that," Rachel says and holds her stomach as she laughs.

I lean on the doorjamb and watch them. My heart catches as Maeve glances at Rachel with affection and humor, and then pats my daughter on the shoulder.

I've never considered what it would look like to have someone else in our lives. Mostly because I had no problem raising Rachel alone. I didn't *need* a woman to complete our family.

But seeing *this* woman, here in our home, laughing and talking with Rachel…it makes me yearn for something new.

Something unexpected.

Something damn sappy.

"Oh, hey," Maeve says when she sees me.

"Where did you go?" Rachel asks. "We heard your car."

"I ran back over to Maeve's to fix her sink."

"You did?" Maeve asks with round, green eyes. "You didn't have to do that. It was so stinky."

"I held my breath." I shrug a shoulder and give her a wink. "It's working now."

"Well, thanks. How much do I owe you?"

I laugh and shake my head. "I think it's a fair trade for your interior design services."

"We found some cool stuff," Rachel informs me. "I just need your credit card."

I raise a brow, but Maeve continues.

"We didn't go too crazy. I think you'll like it. Oh, my phone's ringing." She pulls her cell out of her pocket and scoots off the bed. "I have to take this. I'll be right back."

She slips past me, and I walk over to sit on the bed with my daughter.

"I like her," she says, staring at the doorway. "She's

really nice, and she's easy to talk to. I told her some stuff. And, I have to apologize to you."

"You do?"

"Yeah." She swallows and stares down at her iPad. "I know I've been kind of difficult."

"Kind of?"

"It's just…Maeve says that it's okay for me to screw up sometimes, but I have to apologize if I've hurt someone I love. So, I'm apologizing. Because I know I made you really mad. And kind of sad, too."

"Yeah, I was kind of sad." I brush my hand down her soft hair and wonder when my baby grew up. I lean over and kiss her temple. "Listen, this is a good move for us. A clean slate. You don't hate it, right?"

"I thought I would," she admits. "I wanted to hate it. But the house is awesome, and I like the water. And, someday, I'm getting that apartment above the garage."

I smirk. "I knew you'd love that."

"I'm nervous about school, but Maeve says it'll be okay. That the kids here are pretty nice. And I have the whole summer to get used to it here, and meet some people."

"You had quite a lot to say in the short time I was gone."

She smiles and then looks up when Maeve comes back to the doorway.

"Sorry, guys," Maeve says. "I had to talk a client off the ledge. It happens sometimes."

Rachel's stomach growls next to me, catching my attention.

"Are you two hungry?"

"Uh, yeah. I'm going to die of starvation," Rachel says.

"I could eat," Maeve adds.

"Let's go to the pub for lunch. I know you eat there all the time," I say to Maeve, "but I'd love to show Rachel. Or, we can go somewhere else."

"The pub!" Rachel announces. "After you pay for my new bedroom stuff."

"The pub it is," Maeve says with a laugh. "I think my parents are there today. They just arrived from Ireland a couple of days ago."

"Your parents live in *Ireland*?" Rachel asks as I type my credit card into the iPad. "That's so cool."

"That's right," Maeve says. "But they're here for a while because my sister-in-law is about to have a baby, and they don't want to miss it."

I press purchase on the screen and then tuck my card away. "Okay, ladies, let's go eat."

But they're already ahead of me, walking together and chattering away.

The pub is fairly empty when we arrive as they've just opened for the day.

"You don't work until later," Maggie reminds Maeve as we walk in.

"I'm not here to work," Maeve replies. "I'm here to eat. And to show off the pub to my new friend, Rachel."

"You must be Hunter's daughter," Maggie says with a smile. "You're welcome to sit anywhere you like, as you can see."

"And will you be having a Guinness then?" Keegan asks my daughter with a wink. She smiles, completely charmed by the accent.

"Dad would kill me," she says. "But I'll have a Coke."

"Coming right up," Keegan replies.

"Let's sit at the bar," Rachel decides and climbs up onto a stool. "This place is *so* cool."

Maeve passes us menus. "We think so, too. Izzy, are you okay?"

The pregnant woman comes waddling into the bar, pressing a hand to her back.

"Yeah, I've had these stupid false labor contractions all morning. It's so annoying." Izzy smiles at Rachel. "Hey there, I'm Izzy. That one's wife." She points at Keegan, and Rachel looks almost disappointed.

"You're married?" she asks Keegan.

"Aye, I am, darlin'." He winks at her, and I feel my lips twitch. "But if she ever leaves me, you and I will run off together."

Rachel laughs and sips her Coke, and we order a little bit of everything off the appetizer menu to share.

"Are you sure you're having *false* labor?" I ask Izzy when she scowls and presses her hand to her back once more.

"Yeah, Keegan has rushed me to the doctor several times in the past week. But it's nothing. And I'm still a few weeks out from my due date. The doctor says this is just my body's way of getting ready for the real thing."

"Does it hurt? Having your belly out like that?" Rachel asks.

"It's not comfortable," Izzy replies. "I've become best friends with a bottle of shea butter that I slather all over it all the time so I don't get a ton of stretch marks. And, man, my ankles have never been so swollen in all my life. I'm not even thirty and I have *cankles.* What's that all about?"

"Ew," is all Rachel says.

"Exactly," Izzy agrees.

"Hey, guys," Maeve says to her siblings. "Hunter invited me to go to the ESPYs with him in LA."

"The whatsies?" Maggie asks.

"You know, the prestigious awards show that recognizes excellence in sports," Rachel says.

"Oh, right. Cool." Maggie grins. "That'll be fun."

"I don't have anything to wear," Maeve replies. "And I don't know where to start."

"I do," Izzy announces. "When I needed on-air clothes, Natalie and Jules helped me out."

"Jules McKenna?" I ask.

"Yes, exactly."

"Good idea." I nod.

"He knows Jules?" Izzy asks Maeve, who nods.

"Long story," Maeve says. "Okay, I'll call them. I

don't know them very well. Is it weird to call and ask for fashion advice?"

"Trust me," Izzy assures her, "it's not weird. They *love* this stuff. They are the experts."

Someone turns on the sound system, and Irish music fills the air. There's no live band this early in the day, but Maggie and Maeve begin to sing with the music.

They have beautiful voices, and suddenly, Maggie starts to dance in that fascinating way the Irish do.

"I've always wondered how to do that," Rachel says as she watches with wide eyes.

"Well, come on then. We'll show you," Maeve says and takes Rachel's hand to pull her onto the floor.

The two sisters slow down to show Rachel the steps.

Suddenly, an unfamiliar man comes walking out of the kitchen area and joins the girls with a smile. For an older guy, he sure can move.

"Da loves to charm the ladies," Keegan says as he joins me to watch them. "You haven't met my parents yet, have you?"

"No. I've been busy moving into the house over the past couple of weeks."

Keegan nods and then looks me in the eyes. "I know you have your eye on my sister. And I understand it, as she's a lovely lass. But if you hurt her, my brothers and I will make you suffer for it. It's no matter that you know your way in the ring."

I nod and know in my gut that I'll have the same conversation with any man who has his eye on my daughter someday.

"I would expect nothing less."

"I'm glad we understand each other." Keegan nods and steps back as Izzy joins him behind the counter.

She has to lean against the bar and take a deep breath.

"Izzy, I don't think this is false labor," I inform her. "I'm no expert, but this doesn't look fake at all."

"Doesn't feel fake, but none of it has this week. It just is what it is."

But before she can say anything else, a sploosh of water floods the floor from beneath her maternity dress.

"Well," Izzy says in shock. "I guess I *am* in labor."

"Call an ambulance," Keegan announces, and I immediately reach for my phone and dial 911. Someone cuts off the music, and everyone gathers around.

"Take some deep breaths," Keegan says to his wife, rubbing his hand in a circle over her back.

"I do *not* want to have this baby in a bar," Izzy says between breaths.

"We'll get you to the hospital," Maggie says and then turns to the kitchen, yelling, "Ma! Come quick!"

"What's all the fuss?" An older woman draped in a white apron with red hair just like her daughters' bustles out of the kitchen while wiping her hands on a tea towel. "What's wrong?"

"Izzy's in labor," Maeve says. "Sorry, Hunter, these are my parents, Tom and Fiona. This is Rachel and Hunter."

"Oh, we've heard about you," Fiona says as she sidles up next to her daughter-in-law and takes over rubbing the woman's back. "It's a pleasure to meet you."

"Maybe Rachel and I should go."

"No way, Dad," Rachel says, shaking her head. "I'm not going anywhere. I don't want to miss this."

"You stay right here with me," Tom says with a wink for my daughter.

"Oh, God, I have to push." Izzy meets her husband's gaze with scared eyes. "I seriously don't want to have the baby in the bar. Why is this happening so fast?"

"I suspect you've been in labor all week," Fiona says.

"Let's get her upstairs then," I announce and hurry behind the bar. Keegan takes her head and shoulders, and I lift her legs, and we easily carry her up the stairs to the apartment above. We lay her on the bed, and I make a hasty retreat back downstairs.

"Send the paramedics up when they get here," Maeve says as she and the other women rush past me to help Izzy.

"Is she going to have the baby up there?" Rachel asks when I return to the bar.

"Maybe. I don't know."

"She's in good hands," Tom says calmly. "My Fiona

knows what to do. She had five babies of her own, and has helped plenty others have their wee babes."

"I like to listen to you," Rachel admits to Tom, and the older man smiles gently. "I like your voice."

"It's glad I am to hear it." He pats her shoulder. "Do you want some cake? My Fiona made some, and now that she's busy, we can sneak a bit, you and me."

"I *love* cake. What kind is it?"

"Apple, and it's the best you'll ever have. And that's the truth of it. Come now, we'll get us some."

Tom leads Rachel into the kitchen, and people start coming through the doors.

"What's going on?" Shawn asks as he and Lexi join me. "Maeve called but only said to get our asses over here."

"Izzy's having the baby upstairs."

"*Upstairs?*" Lexi asks. "Holy crap, I'm going up." She tosses her handbag onto the bar and hurries to the stairs.

"I have no interest in going up there," Shawn says with a shudder. "I don't care if that makes me a coward. I'll stay here and be moral support from afar. Kane and Anastasia are on their way over."

"Why isn't the ambulance here?" I ask but hear sirens in the distance. "Ah, here they come."

"It can take a while around here," Shawn says. "It's bloody annoying."

Paramedics rush in, and we direct them upstairs.

And then it's quiet. We hear voices, footsteps rushing above us.

Maeve runs down. "It's too late to move her. She's pushing. It's going to be a bit, and then they'll take her to the hospital."

And with that, she runs back up.

I blow out a breath and decide to check in on my daughter and Tom. Before I can push through the swinging kitchen door, I can hear them talking.

"You were a wee bit short with your da out there," Tom says.

"I didn't say anything bad to him," Rachel replies.

"It's not *what* you said, but how you said it," Tom says.

"I guess I get frustrated with him sometimes. Or, a lot of the time. He's just so strict. So…*bossy*. Like I'm not old enough to make my own decisions or something."

"How old are ye then? Thirty?"

"No, I'm fifteen."

"Ah, that's a good age, and that's for sure. But, you're not fully grown yet, and your da's just trying to be a good father. I know because I'm a da meself, and I raised five babies. I have to admit, if my kids spoke to me that way, even today, it would hurt my feelings."

"Your feelings?"

"Of course. Because I love them, and I wouldn't speak to someone I love like that. What if you didn't *have* your da anymore? If something happened to him?"

"Well, that would be awful."

"Indeed it would. I've always said, we should treat those we love as though we're not guaranteed tomorrow with them. Because we aren't."

"I guess you're right. I'll do better."

"That's all anyone can ask. Now, should we have another piece of this cake?"

I walk away before either of them knows I was there. I don't know if that talk will help with Rachel's tone when it comes to me, but it can't hurt.

Just as I join the other guys at the bar, Izzy screams.

"Jesus," I mutter and rub my hand over my face, as nervous as I was when Rachel was born.

"Yeah." Shawn swallows hard. "Didn't need to hear that."

Suddenly, Maeve comes rushing down, smiling widely. "It's a girl. A perfect little girl. They're looking everyone over and getting them ready to transport to the hospital so they can be checked out. But I think everything went just beautifully."

Her eyes fill with tears, and I tug her over to me.

"I'm glad to hear it, Doctor Maeve."

She smacks me on the arm but laughs. "She's such a tiny little thing."

"Women always get all bent out of shape over babies," Shawn says, shaking his head, but his expression is soft. "I want to see them before they leave."

"What did we miss?" Anastasia asks as she and Kane hurry through the door. "What's going on?"

"Izzy had the baby *upstairs*," Maeve announces. "A little girl."

"Wow, that was fast," Anastasia says. "Hi, Hunter."

This is the most entertainment I've had in months.

"Hey there."

"Are they okay, then?" Kane asks, his accent almost as thick as his father's.

"As far as we know, yes," Maeve says. "It just happened so quickly. Ma thinks Izzy's been laboring for several days."

"I think she's been in labor all week," I add. "Just based on what she said a few minutes ago. But I'm not a doctor. I could be wrong."

"As long as she's okay. And the baby is healthy," Anastasia says, and we all turn as the EMTs bring Izzy and the baby downstairs.

Tom and Rachel hurry out of the kitchen, and Tom leans in to kiss Izzy's cheek and rub his fingertip across the baby's head.

"Blessings to you, my darlin' girls."

We follow as a group while the little family is loaded into the ambulance.

"Take care of my pub," Keegan yells out at us, the biggest smile on his face. "I'm a da!"

"What a big goof," Maggie says but wipes a tear from her eye. "Thank God for Ma. If you weren't here, things could have been bad."

"But I was here, my darlin'." Fiona wraps her arm

around her daughter. "Now, let's go inside. I'll cut into the apple cake I made."

"We already cut into it," Rachel says, and Tom shakes his head mournfully.

"Tom O'Callaghan," Fiona says sternly. "You know I said to wait."

"It was what the Americans call *stress eating*. I was just a wee bit worried about all of my girls up there."

"Bollocks," Fiona says. "Come, now. We'll eat what's left and anything else that anyone wants. We have a new grandbabe."

Once back inside, the music starts again, and there's laughter and celebration as the O'Callaghans celebrate their new addition.

Rachel's managed to situate herself right in the middle of it all. Not shy in the least, she's eating food and dancing with the girls. Laughing.

My baby is laughing and acting like a *kid*. Something I haven't seen in far too long.

It seems the O'Callaghans are good for both of us.

I catch Maeve by the hand as she sweeps past me and lead her down the hall to a private corner. When I'm sure we're out of sight of the others, I close my mouth over hers in a long, sweet kiss that has me wanting far more.

"What was that for?" she asks with a smile.

"I just needed it." I kiss her forehead. "It felt like the right moment."

"Well, I'm not complaining at all. I'm glad you were here. It made all of the craziness even more fun."

"Rachel's having the time of her life."

"And you?"

I tuck a lock of her auburn hair behind her ear. "There's nowhere else I'd rather be. But I have to tell you, your family is a bit crazy."

She laughs and pats me on the cheek. "You don't know the half of it."

CHAPTER 7

"Are you *sure* it wasn't completely crazy that I called you guys? I mean, we don't know each other all that well, and I don't mean to put anyone out."

"This is what we were born to do," Jules says, her face completely serious. "Tell her, Stasia."

"She means it," Anastasia assures me. "Jules and Nat are the bee's knees when it comes to fashion."

"We like to shop," Natalie says with a smile. "Like, if shopping were an Olympic sport, Jules and I would be tied for first place."

"No, we would *be* first place because we're a team, and shopping is a team sport," Jules says with a laugh. "Okay, now let's get serious here. Nat, do you have any chocolate cheesecake?"

"Duh." Natalie rolls her eyes. "But you don't get any until we've found the perfect dress for Maeve."

She turns to me with excitement burning in her green eyes. Natalie is gorgeous, with long, dark hair and a curvy figure. Jules is just as beautiful, but where Natalie is dark, Jules is fair—much like her cousin, Anastasia.

"We called in a couple of designers to bring some dresses," Natalie informs me. "This is a *televised* event, and Hunter is a big deal in the sports world. You'll want to look your absolute best."

I swallow hard, already intimidated. I guess I *knew* that he was a big deal, but he's just Hunter to me. The hot guy I'm more than a little interested in. But for that evening, he'll be Hunter Meyers, superstar fighter.

Will he be the same person? Will I *like* him? Will I make a fool out of myself, and in turn, him?

"I'm thrilled for you," Jules adds, pulling me out of my reverie. "For both of you, really. I've known Hunter for a long time, and I have so many questions. But I don't want to sound too nosy."

Nat and Stasia both smirk.

"What? I'm *not* a gossip."

"Oh, for the love of God, stop lying to the woman," Nat says with a laugh.

"You can ask me pretty much anything you want." I wink at Jules, who grins in return, but before she can say anything, Nat jumps right to the task at hand.

"Let's get you into some dresses, and *then* we can talk all about the hot fighter," Nat suggests and rushes over to a doorway, whispering something to the designer or assistant or whoever in the hell is in the other room. Then, she crosses back to me, and a woman follows with a rack of gowns. "I hope you don't have any issues getting mostly naked in front of us because it's just faster for you to get in and out of the gowns if you don't have to dash away between each one."

"I'm good to go. I have sisters," I remind her and whip my shirt over my head, shimmying out of my jeans to stand before them in my strapless bra and panties. "Let's do this."

"Wow," Stasia says, her eyebrows raised. She lets out a low whistle. "You're hot, Maeve."

"I was just going to say…you have the most amazing boobs," Jules agrees. "Hunter's a lucky guy. I bet he loves your boobs, too."

"He hasn't seen them," I mutter and then look up to find them all staring at me in surprise. "What?"

"He hasn't *seen* them?" Jules repeats. "And he invited you to the ESPYs?"

"Yeah." I bite my lower lip. "Is that bad?"

"That's *amazing*," Jules replies. "Okay, let's start with the red."

"No red," Nat disagrees. "I think she'd look amazing in green."

I smile. Everyone always thinks redheads look good in green.

Then again, they aren't wrong.

"I'd also like to try that white one," I add, pointing to a long, white dress that looks amazing on the hanger.

"You can try them all," Nat reminds me. "Let's start."

She pulls down the white one first and helps me step into it. But when it's zipped up, and I look in the mirror, I shake my head.

"It bunches weird around my stomach," I say, pointing to the offending area. "It looks...off."

"Agreed. No bunching, and no ruching." Anastasia points to the purple gown. "That one. I want to see it."

"Okay, while I'm your personal Barbie to dress up as you like, feel free to ask questions, Jules."

"Awesome. First of all, Hunter's fantastic. I mean, yeah, he's a badass fighter, and he scares people because that's his job, but he's *so* nice. And Rachel is just the sweetest."

"She's been giving him a hard time, but I agree. She's great."

"How did you meet him?" Jules asks.

"I sold him a house on the island." I fill them in on Rachel's behavior lately, and how Hunter wants a small-town life for her. "Even though he'd already chosen a house, he kept asking me to show him more. I thought he was a jerk who just wanted to look at everything we have listed, but he admitted that he wanted to see more of me."

All three women stare at me again and then sigh.

"That may be the sweetest thing I've ever heard," Natalie says. "I thought *my* husband was sweet."

"Your husband *is* sweet," Jules says. "So, you've only known Hunter for a few weeks."

"I guess so," I agree. "Not quite a month yet. Do you think it's moving fast?"

"I think these things should move as quickly as you're comfortable with them moving," Stasia says. "Kane and I didn't know each other very long before we knew we were in love."

"I didn't say *love*." The words are quickly out of my mouth. "That's not what I meant."

"Not yet," Jules says with a wink. "Okay, that's not working. Let's try the green. Now, I get to tell *you* some stuff about Hunter."

"Oh, do tell. I mean, if it turns out he's a big jerk, I'd rather know now *before* I go to LA with him."

"I already told you, he's awesome," Jules says with a laugh and zips up the strapless dress, then steps back and taps her lips as we both look in the mirror.

"Whoa," Stasia says.

"Gorgeous," Nat adds.

I just stare at the woman looking back at me in the mirror. This dress hugs my curves perfectly but doesn't make me look fat. And the green really is great with my hair and eyes.

"Okay, this is the one." I turn and look at my back-side in the mirror. "It even makes my ass look great."

"Hunter's going to swallow his tongue," Jules agrees. "You're ridiculously sexy, Maeve."

She's not wrong.

"What were you going to tell me?" I ask her.

"Oh, right. I know that what's in the past doesn't really matter, but Hunter doesn't date. He doesn't take women to awards shows. He's *never* been photographed with anyone. He always said that he didn't want his daughter to look at images of him online when she got older, only to see him with a different woman in each of the photos."

"Okay, that's… I don't even know what that is, but it's totally swoony," Nat decides and props her hands on her hips.

"And something Luke would have done," Jules points out.

"So, the fact that he's taking you to this event and introduced you to Rachel, tells me that you mean something to him. And I just think that's pretty awesome."

"He can't possibly have been celibate for the past fifteen years," I say.

"No, I'd say not. But he's discreet and discerning. He's a professional. And he's a good guy."

"Yeah, he's a good guy," I agree and turn back to look at myself in the mirror. "I don't want to take off this dress."

"Here's one word of advice," Jules says as she steps up beside me and holds my gaze in the mirror. "Maybe, if you feel comfortable, when you *do* wear this dress, let him be the one to peel you out of it. Because holy shit. Once he unwraps you from this, he's going to rock your world."

"I should hope so," I whisper. "Wait, I don't know if I can buy it. There aren't price tags on these dresses."

"Oh, that's on purpose," Nat says, waving me off. "Hunter has it covered. We also have some shoes for you to choose, and he'll have a stylist on hand in LA to do your hair and makeup."

I stare at them, certain I've misheard. "Well, holy shit. He doesn't have to do that."

"He wants to," Jules says. "He was excited about it when he called me. Let him do it. It's sweet."

I glance over when Stasia sniffles. "What's wrong?"

"It's just so great." She wipes at a tear. "And you totally deserve to be spoiled like this. It's awesome, isn't it? To have a sexy guy think you're the shit and spoil you with fun things and all of that happy stuff."

"It's…disconcerting. And, yeah, a little awesome."

We narrow the shoes down to a black pair that goes well with the dress and that I can wear with other things later. They have a red sole.

I never, in a million years, thought I'd own a pair of red-soled shoes.

Then, we make our way to the kitchen, and Natalie pulls a cheesecake out of the fridge.

"Just a small piece for me," I tell her, already thinking about the fit of that dress and how I don't want to gain any weight before I have to fit myself into it.

"Oh, honey, we don't slice it up." She takes out four forks and passes them out. "We just dig in."

"Aren't they great?" Stasia asks with a wide smile before scooping up a big bite and shoveling it into her mouth. "These girls know how to live."

"I think I've fallen in love with *you guys*. I mean, who needs men when you have gorgeous clothes and cheesecake?"

"Exactly," Jules says. "Though I'm rather fond of other things that Nate offers as well. Still, this is hard to beat."

"Thank you. For everything today," I say as I take a bite of the best chocolate cheesecake I've ever had. "I'm still nervous to go, but at least I know I'll look good."

"Oh, it's completely our pleasure," Jules assures me. "And we can't wait to hear all about it."

"I think we'll need a girls' night after Maeve gets back to town," Nat says. "So she can tell us everything."

"Agreed," Stasia says.

"I'm in," I reply. "Can we do it on the island so Izzy can come? She just had the baby and isn't going far yet. But I know she won't want to miss it."

"I love that island," Jules says. "I think Nate and I should buy a weekend place there."

"Don't you have the beach house down the coast?" Stasia asks.

"Well, yeah, but it's *the island*."

I laugh. "I'd be happy to sell you something. Just let me know when you want to look."

"You know, we could all come over to the island, the couples, and stay in vacation rentals or something," Nat says, thinking it over. "Us girls could have our night, and the guys could hang at the pub. And then maybe you and Nate can look for real estate."

"You know I love to multi-task," Jules says, thinking it over. "And I love this idea. Let's plan it."

"The island won't know what hit it," I say, already excited.

THE STORM OUTSIDE IS *CRAZY*. Because we're surrounded by water, it's not unusual for rain to come in and stay for a while, but this storm came out of nowhere, and it's a doozy.

The wind howls and is probably wreaking havoc on my roof. I've known that I need to replace it for a couple of seasons, but I thought I'd be buying my dream house soon.

"I guess the roof's back on my list," I mutter and then jump when lightning explodes, and thunder rails against the house. "Jesus, this is nuts."

Suddenly, as if a faucet has flipped on, water starts pouring in through the ceiling of my bedroom, right *onto* the beautiful dress I'm supposed to wear in less than forty-eight hours.

Why did this storm wait until the *day* I brought the dress home to decide to destroy my house?

"Oh, my God." I jump out of bed and tug on a sweatshirt and sweatpants, staring helplessly as my room floods. "What do I do?"

I reach for my phone and try to figure out who to call.

It's after three in the morning.

I can't call Keegan—I don't want to wake the baby.

I could call Kane.

"Wait, no. I don't want to wake *their* baby, either. Why are there so many babies?"

I rush down the stairs and listen to the roar of the water coming into my house.

I'm sick to my stomach.

"Shawn." I tap my screen and listen to the phone ring. "Come on, pick up."

"'Lo?"

"It's me. I need help."

"What's wrong?" I can hear that he's instantly awake and sitting up in bed.

"My house is flooding. It's like there's a river coming through my ceiling. I don't know what to do."

"Do you have ladders?"

"Yeah, a couple. In the garage."

"I'll be there in ten."

He hangs up, and I'm on the verge of tears when I realize that there's absolutely *no* way I can go to LA the day after tomorrow.

So, without thinking, I dial Hunter's number.

"Maeve?" he asks, his voice full of sleep. "Are you okay?"

I have to swallow my tears and try to sound sane and rational. "Hi. I'm sorry to inform you that I won't be able to accompany you to LA. I hope you have a lovely trip."

"Wait, wha—?"

I hang up quickly because I'm near hysterics.

Where is Shawn? The water is starting to come down the stairs now.

Finally, I hear banging on my front door. When I open it, not only is Shawn there, but more cars are pulling in.

"Jesus, what's going on?" Kane asks as he hurries out of his Porsche. Keegan comes to a screeching halt behind Kane.

Maggie and Lexi rush up my driveway, and even Ma and Da climb out of Shawn's car.

"What are you all doing here? I just called Shawn."

"Don't you know," Keegan says, "when you call one, you call us all. We're a damn phone tree."

"What's he doing here?" Maggie asks, pointing to Cameron, who I'm just as shocked to see.

"Don't you know?" he says, echoing Keegan. "We're a phone tree."

Maggie rolls her eyes and keeps her distance from Cameron as Da climbs my porch steps.

"What's happening in there?" Da asks and pushes his way through the front door, coming to a stop at the sight of the river of water making its way down my stairway. "Oh, for the love of all the saints. You have a mess on your hands here, Maeve, me love."

"I know." Tears threaten once again. "I don't know what to do."

"Is that Hunter?" Maggie asks, pointing to the car parking down the block, and the figure running from it toward my house.

I'd recognize him anywhere.

"What in the hell is going on?" he demands when he gets up to my porch, pushing his way through the others.

"I have a catastrophe on my hands," I reply and gesture to all of the water. My brothers are running about, deciding what to do. "And the beautiful dress, *my* beautiful dress that you gave me, is ruined. I can't just leave. I don't have anything to wear anymore."

"Okay. Okay, take a breath." He doesn't even care that my *entire* family is here. He just pulls me into his arms and hugs me tightly.

"Is that Hunter Meyers?" I hear Cameron ask as he climbs the stairs with Kane. "What in the hell? I've been gone too long."

"That's Cameron," I say against Hunter's chest. "He's a good friend of the family. Kane's best friend. And I think he's in love with my sister."

Hunter kisses my head. "I'll introduce myself to him when we're hanging tarps outside. Are you okay? I'm going to help the guys and get this water taken care of."

"Oh, you don't—"

"She's good," Maggie assures him and takes my hand as he hurries off to join the other guys. "I really like him."

"Yeah." I swallow the tears and brush at my face. "He's kind of great."

"Did you see his arms?" she whispers in my ear.

"Girl, I've been looking at those arms for *weeks*. It was nice of Cameron to come help."

She shrugs a shoulder. "Yeah. It was."

But that's all she says. We all huddle in my wet living room, my ma, Lexi, Maggie, and me, as the guys shout orders at each other, climb ladders, and throw ropes and tarps.

"I don't want Da on a ladder," I mutter and shudder at the thought of him falling. "Definitely not in this rain. And it's dark outside."

"He's handled worse than this," Ma assures me. Suddenly, the river down my stairs slows to a trickle. "Looks like they covered the hole."

"Everything's ruined." My voice sounds hollow as I stare at my original hardwood floors. "What a mess."

"There are water restoration people we can call in the morning," Maggie says, patting my back.

"It *is* the morning."

"You know what I mean."

"I think that's all we can do for tonight," Kane says as he and Cam walk downstairs, and the others come in from outside. "It'll at least help to stop more water from getting in. But you can't stay tonight, lass. It's not safe."

"She'll come home with me," Hunter announces.

Silence falls.

My brothers, father, and Cam all look at each other, then cross their arms over their chests and turn to Hunter.

"Is that so, then?" Da asks, his voice as cold as I've ever heard it.

"I hate to interrupt this testosterone standoff, but given that I'm a grown woman, I'll decide where I'm staying."

I grin as all of the eyes in the room turn to me.

"I'll go stay with Hunter. He has room, and it's not far from here."

"You'll do well to mind your manners," Da warns but then pats Hunter on the shoulder as he walks past him.

Everyone files out of the house, and I just stand there for a moment, unsure what to do next.

"We should go get dry," Hunter suggests, his hands on my shoulders.

"I can't even take much with me," I say. "It's all wet. I have my purse. I guess I could go gather some makeup and my toothbrush."

"In the morning," he says and kisses my head.

"Come on, let's go to my place and get warm. Wait here. I'll go get the car."

He runs down the block to his car, and I lock the door, then wait on the porch as he pulls into the driveway.

"I don't want to sit in that gorgeous seat in these wet clothes, Hunter."

"It'll be okay. Honest."

I sit down, wince, and try to keep my ass off the seat while he drives.

It's a seriously good core workout.

"Sit," he says.

"No. My ass is wet. This car is worth more than my *house*."

"It's just a fucking car," he says, but there's no censure in his voice.

"We're almost there."

He pulls into the garage, and I get out of the car.

"I'm staying in the apartment upstairs," I inform him.

"Why?"

"Because." I take a deep breath, too tired and too emotionally exhausted to play coy. "You have a teenage daughter in your house. I'm too attracted to you, too damn into you, to keep my hands to myself. So, I'm going to stay out here. Because I'm not in my right mind tonight, and I was raised better than to attack you when your little girl is here."

His eyes flare. His hands fist.

"Fucking hell, you disarm me," he mutters. "Okay. Let's go, then. And, Maeve, neither of us is going to be keeping our hands to ourselves for much longer."

"Promise?"

CHAPTER 8

"**Y**ou want *what?*" I hear on the other end of the line.

"I need the dress remade." I mix my protein shake by hand. "It was ruined last night by a flood. And I need it, in LA, by tomorrow at noon."

"Mr. Meyers, it's a one-of-a-kind dress. I don't just have another hanging around here that I can send to you."

"I need it," I repeat. "I'm happy to pay for it. Look, it wasn't her fault. It was an act of God. And I'll be damned if she doesn't wear the dress she fell in love with."

There's a pause on the other end, and then a sigh. "Okay. I'll make it happen."

"Thank you."

I end the call and turn when I hear bare feet pad into the kitchen.

"Good morning." I take a sip of my shake. "Did you hear me come and go in the middle of the night?"

Rachel frowns. "You snuck out?"

"Honey, I'm the boss around here. I don't ever *sneak.* I left."

My daughter yawns and then reaches for a box of cereal. "Didn't hear you. Where'd you go?"

"I had to help Maeve."

That wakes her up. "Is she okay?"

"Yeah, but her house isn't. She's staying in the apartment above the garage."

"Oh my God, Dad. Why didn't you say something sooner?"

I raise a brow. "You were sleeping."

Rachel pours two cups of coffee, doctors them up with too much sugar, and starts to leave.

"Where are you going?"

"To comfort Maeve," she says like I should already know the answer to that stupid question.

I grin. I love that my daughter likes Maeve. Hell, she likes the whole family. And what's not to like? They're a bunch of awesome people.

Watching how they all rallied around Maeve last night only cemented for me the fact that these are the kind of people I want in our lives, and I've only known these people for roughly a month. It's unexpected but only reaffirms that moving here is precisely what Rachel and I needed.

I pour my own cup of coffee, black, and walk out to the apartment.

When I enter, both girls are sitting at the small table by the kitchenette, sipping their drinks.

"Good morning," I say and watch in horror as Maeve's eyes fill with tears. "Hey, what did I do?"

"Nothing." She wipes the tears and blows out a breath.

"She's just emotional," Rachel explains. "It's been a rough night."

"Did you get any sleep?" I ask Maeve as I sit next to her.

"Not really." She sighs and checks the time. I feel like shit. I should have stayed with her last night. "I'm just waiting for people to open up for the day so I can start making calls. I'm sorry about the trip. I know it's short notice."

"Hey, Rach, why don't you go get some breakfast?"

She frowns, but I give my head a brief shake, and she nods.

"Oh, yeah. Sure. I could eat."

Rachel takes her mug and leaves the apartment. When I can no longer hear her clomping down the steps, I reach over to push a stray piece of hair behind Maeve's ear.

"You're still going to LA, babe."

Maeve frowns. "I don't see how."

"Well, you have a million relatives who will be

happy to oversee things at the house for a couple of days. We won't even be gone a full forty-eight hours."

"But the dress—"

"Has been dealt with." I sip my coffee. "It's all been handled."

"Hunter, I don't even have *underwear* at this point."

"Yes, you do. I'm crazy about you, but you're being dramatic, Maeve. We just have to go gather your stuff, bring it back here, and run it through the laundry. Good as new. We gather up any toiletries you need—or buy new ones. I have so much luggage, I could open my own shop, so you're covered there."

She bites her lip, and I see a little spark of hope light in those gorgeous eyes.

"I guess my clothes aren't *ruined*," she admits. "Just wet."

"Yep. Clothes can be saved from the wetness. We just have to go get them before they mold."

Her eyes widen. "*Mold.* Oh, God, I'm going to have mold in my house."

"No, you're not. Because we're going to call people to come take care of it. It's a pisser, I won't deny it, but it's all fixable. The most important thing is that *you* are safe, Maeve. You're the only thing that can't be replaced."

She nods, sighs, and then firms that bottom lip. "Okay, enough of this wallowing. It's dumb and doesn't solve anything. I'm just tired. Because you're right, all of this can be dealt with. Can you give me a lift over to my place so I can gather up some stuff? And if you don't mind, I might have to camp out here in this apartment for a little while."

"You're welcome here for as long as you like."

I don't think it's wise to tell her she can stay forever. Not yet.

And I need to have a conversation with my kid because I have no intention of letting Maeve stay out above the garage for long.

"Of course. We'll take the bigger car."

"You have a bigger car?"

I smile at her. "Several."

"You're a car guy, aren't you?"

"I do enjoy a well-built automobile, yes."

She smirks. "You and Kane are two peas in a pod. I'm ready when you are."

"Let's go, then. I'll let Rachel know we're leaving."

"Do you trust her here alone?"

I raise a brow. "Where is she going to go? We're on an island. But, yes, she seems to have turned over a new leaf and hasn't pulled any bullshit since we got here. Granted, it hasn't been that long, but so far, so good."

"I'm glad," she says as she follows me down the stairs. "She's a sweetheart. She was so worried when she brought me coffee this morning."

"She's a good kid," I agree.

Rachel insists on going with us to help, so I decide to take the bigger Range Rover. When we turn the corner, and Maeve's house comes into view, Rachel gasps.

"Holy crap," my daughter mutters.

"It looks worse in the light of day," Maeve agrees. "How did you guys get those tarps up there in the rain *and* the dark?"

It was a bitch and a half.

"We're men," I say and pull to a stop in the driveway. "We have our ways."

"Well, thank God for *your ways* because there's no way I could have done that on my own."

We get out of the car, and Rachel and I follow Maeve up onto the porch and then inside the house. There's water all over the floors, and when we get upstairs, the hole in the ceiling of the master bedroom is gaping and still dripping.

There's a green blob of material on the floor beneath it that I assume used to be a dress.

"This must have been scary," Rachel says and reaches for Maeve's hand. "I'm so sorry."

"Scared the hell out of me," Maeve agrees. "Okay, I'm just going to pack a couple of suitcases with most of my clothes and some toiletries. I don't think the bathroom was flooded too badly."

She pulls some luggage out of a hall closet, and we all get to work helping her fill them with sopping clothes after stuffing them into trash bags.

"Oh, my jewelry box, too," Maeve adds and tugs it out of the closet. "And my important papers. I have them all in one filing box. I'm sure they'd be safe here, but I'd feel better if the important stuff was with me."

"Understandable," I reply and start to haul things out to the Rover. Less than an hour after we walked into the house, Maeve is locking it up again, and we're headed back to my place.

"You only have four suitcases of clothes," Rachel says as we begin to haul everything up to the apartment. "How is that possible?"

Maeve laughs. "I'm not really a collector of *things*. I'm definitely not a clothes horse. I have nice things, and when I'm done with them, I donate them. My wardrobe is always evolving, and I don't hang on to much."

"I still have clothes that I wore in junior high," my daughter replies.

"I'm so glad there's a washer and dryer up here," Maeve says as she begins opening her cases and tossing items into piles. "It'll make it easier. When do we leave tomorrow?"

"You're going?" Rachel asks, excitement on her young face.

"We're going," I confirm. "We'll drop Rach off at my parents' by nine and meet the plane at ten. We have to be on the red carpet by six."

"Well, then, I'd better get busy."

∽

"THIS IS FANCY." Maeve runs her hands over the soft leather of her seat and looks out the window at the view. We're somewhere over central California. She's sitting across from me, facing forward. I'm in the seat directly across from her so I can look at her. "You own a private plane?"

I grin. "No. I charter it."

"You know, you didn't have to do all of this just for me. You don't have to impress me."

"I usually travel like this. It's easier." I tip my head to the side and take her in. "Does my money make you uncomfortable?"

"I just don't want you to think that you have to do expensive things for me to make me like you. I'm not like that."

No. She's not. And that's why she's here with me.

Well, one of the reasons.

"And I'm not trying to impress you with money." I lean forward and brace my elbows on my knees. "Maeve, I know you don't look things up on the internet, which is actually kind of endearing and nice, but it also means that I have to spell some things out for you. I have more money than I could ever spend in my lifetime."

Her eyes go wide for a moment, and then she blinks and looks down.

I move onto my knees, closer to her, and tip that chin up so she's looking at me with those stunning green eyes.

"I've never really done it in the past, but it turns out that I enjoy spoiling someone. Spoiling *you.*"

"Has there really been no one in your life since Rachel's mom?" The question is quiet and completely without judgment.

"No one important," I reply. "There's been no time and no desire for it. Until you."

"Why me?"

She swallows hard and licks her lips.

God, I fucking want her more than I want my next breath.

"Because the second I saw you, I knew my life was about to change."

Her lips twitch into a smile, and she reaches out to brush her fingers through my hair. "It turns out, Hunter Meyers is charming."

"Not usually, no." I take that hand and kiss her palm. "Are you telling me you didn't feel the chemistry?"

"I felt it," she admits softly. "I didn't know what to do about it. You took me by surprise."

I lean in and press my lips to hers, feeling everything in me tighten, the way it always does when I touch her. "Same goes."

I blindly reach over and press the do not disturb button and then rise on my knees to cup her face as I kiss the hell out of her. She fists those small hands in my shirt, and the low moan from her throat makes my cock twitch.

"I'm going to do things to you," I inform her as I

drag my lips along her jawline, "that you won't soon forget."

"Oh, I have no doubts."

The backs of my fingers brush down over her collarbone and farther still to gently touch the tips of her already perky nipples, straining against her bra.

"You can always say no," I remind her and press a kiss to her chest bone as I unbutton her shirt. "Always."

"So noted." Her fingers delve into my hair again after her shirt is completely open, and I slide it down her arms to toss onto my abandoned chair. Rather than strip her out of her bra, I take my time, slipping one strap over the ball of her shoulder and then pressing a kiss to the smooth skin there.

"I feel like we've been doing the foreplay thing *forever*," she says with a sigh and tilts her head to the side when I drag my lips over to her neck. I take my time enjoying her. I'm able to unfasten her bra with one hand—a skill I acquired in high school—and her heavy breasts spill into my hands.

She sighs.

I groan.

"Too long," I agree. "But it's a damn fine form of torture. I don't mind waiting. I'm not a randy twenty-year-old who can't keep his dick in check."

"How fortunate for both of us." She laughs when I pinch her nipple, and then moans again when I slide my hand into her pants. "If I'd known this would happen on the plane, I would have worn a dress."

"Now we know for next time." I wink at her, urging her pants over her hips, and then sit back and stare at the absolutely stunning woman sitting mostly naked before me. "Fucking Jesus, Maeve."

Curves. That's all I can think as my hands roam over her slightly rounded thighs, the gentle dip of her waist. She has the body of a goddamn goddess.

"I don't work out like I should."

"Did you think that was a complaint?" My eyes meet hers, and I hurry forward to cup her face again and kiss her hard. "You're so fucking beautiful, my eyes hurt. Jesus, it's a good thing I didn't know what you had hidden beneath those clothes because I would have stripped you bare in one of those houses and fucked you on someone's kitchen counter."

Her chuckle is startled and pleased, and I can't help myself.

I grip her by the knees and scoot her forward so I can spread her wide and fucking enjoy her.

"I like the panties, babe." I kiss her navel as I pull the black lace down her legs, and they join the pile of clothes on my chair. "But Christ on a cracker, the view is so much more spectacular without them."

She's not self-conscious in the least, splayed before me.

There's nothing sexier than a confident woman.

She bites her index finger and watches as I kiss her hip and the top of her thigh. Then I hitch one leg over my shoulder and drag a finger through the wet, gorgeous slit that's just begging for my mouth.

"Oh, my," she murmurs.

I grin, lower my head, and just barely lick the edge of her lips.

"Ah, shit," She grips onto my hair, her fingers clutching as I sink in and go to town, lapping her up. I take turns, teasing that little nub of a clit and then feasting on her pussy.

And when I slide a finger inside her, I'm rewarded with her pulsing climax.

She twists in the seat, cries out, and then almost jackknifes into a sitting position.

I feel the plane begin to descend as she stares down at me with shining green eyes.

"Better get dressed." I kiss her thigh, her stomach, each breast. And then I find her lips with mine.

"You're *stopping?*"

"We're about to land." I grin and then kiss her again. "Pretty sure the crew doesn't want to wait while I have my way with you."

"Damn it." But she laughs and reaches for her panties. "That was fun, though."

"Best time I've had in years." I grab her shirt and wrap it around her shoulders, help her into it, and then fasten the buttons. Her eyes never leave mine. "There are always parties after the show. We're not going."

She quirks a brow. "We're not?"

"No. They're boring as hell. It's just a way to see and be seen. And, frankly, I don't give a rat's ass about that."

"Okay, what do you care about?"

"Getting you back to our suite and picking up where we left off."

I slide back into my seat and buckle my belt in time for landing. When the plane slows and begins to taxi toward the terminal, I grin at her.

"Unless you had your heart set on going to the after-parties."

"You know," she says, her voice light and nonchalant, "I was never one for parties. I prefer to spend my time focused on one person. Especially when the party in question is full of people I don't know. Small talk is so…boring."

"Good." I laugh and shake my head. "I do enjoy you, Maeve O'Callaghan."

"The feeling's mutual, Mr. Meyers."

~MAEVE~

"Thanks," Hunter says to the bellhop after we're shown to our suite. He tips him, and we're left alone to explore this gorgeous room.

Actually, *room* is too simple a term for what this is. It's just...massive. It might be bigger than my *house*.

There are two bedrooms *and* two full bathrooms, one on each side of a great room, complete with a kitchen and dining room. The balcony looks out over the city, and I can only imagine how gorgeous it'll be after dark.

But it's the dress that catches my eye.

"My gown," I murmur and cross to it. It's on a dress form in the corner of the room. There's a table set up with hair and makeup supplies. And on the end of the table, closest to me, is a large white box with a red bow tied neatly on top.

"That's for you," Hunter says as he joins me from

behind. He rests his hands on my shoulders and kisses my neck. "Go ahead and open it."

"Hunter, this entire trip is a gift. From the dress to the jet to this room."

"You're too easy to please." He turns me toward him and smiles down at me. "I told you, I'm enjoying myself. Open it."

I pull the lid off the white box and find another *blue* box inside.

The kind of blue box that has a white bow and *Tiffany* written on top.

I glance at Hunter. He's not looking at the box. He's looking at *me*—with the most intense gaze I've ever seen.

I wonder if this is how he looks at an opponent in the ring. Because if so, I would just forfeit.

"You're a little scary, you know that?"

"I can be," he agrees, and when he sighs, his jaw clenches. "But you will never have a reason to be afraid of me, Maeve."

Oh, I'm fairly certain he's wrong about that.

Not because I think he would ever hurt me. Not physically, at least.

But, holy shit, I'm falling in love with this man. And it has nothing at all to do with all of these amazing gifts, and everything to do with the way he looks at me.

How he touches me.

Speaks to me.

"Aren't you going to open it?"

I bite my lip and lift the blue box, unwrap the bow, and remove the lid.

Inside is a black velvet case.

"So many boxes," I murmur with a nervous grin.

When I slide the lid open and see what's inside, I push it into Hunter's hands, shaking my head and stepping back as if it were a snake ready to bite.

"I can't, Hunter. That's too much."

He calmly lifts the chain out of the black velvet, drapes it over his fingers, and holds it up to the light.

"Jules gave me the heads-up that the dress was green. And it's fucking amazing, Maeve. I can't wait to see it on you. Ever since I saw your gorgeous green eyes, I knew I wanted you in emeralds."

He unclasps the chain and walks toward me, but I shake my head again.

"That emerald is the size of my pinky toe," I say.

"Yeah, I wanted to start small."

I let out a startled laugh. "*Small?* Jesus, Hunter, it's *huge.*"

He grins, and I see the line running through his head.

That's what she said.

"I'm serious, that is too much."

"The thing with a gift," he says, still calm as can be, "is that it's not up to the receiver to decide what's too much. It's up to the giver."

I press my lips together as he loops the chain around my neck. Once fastened, the stone falls between my breasts, just above where the dress's neckline will be.

"God, you take my breath away," he whispers. "And later, after I strip you out of that stellar gown, I want to make love to you while you wear this and *only* this."

My breath comes faster. My mouth is beyond dry. I thought I was monumentally turned on in the plane, but this might top that.

"You're good with words," I whisper against his mouth.

"Only because I mean them."

This kiss is long and slow, but before he can take it any further, the doorbell chimes.

"They're here to get you ready," he says and pulls back. But before walking to the door, he lightly touches the emerald on my chest. "You'll want to take a shower before you get started."

"Where will you be?"

"In the other bedroom, getting dressed and briefed on some specifics for tonight. I'll be in and out if you like."

"I kind of like the idea of you seeing me once I'm all put together."

He grins. "That works, too. But I'll be here if you need me."

He kisses my cheek, crosses to the door, and then all hell breaks loose.

Six people come storming inside. It looks like a herd of elephants, and they're all headed toward me.

They tell me their names, but I'll never remember them all.

"Your skin is dull," is the first thing said. "But don't worry, we'll brighten you up. You go shower, do *not* wash your hair, and we'll get set up out here."

"Okay." I start to back away. "Uh, I'll be out soon."

I lock myself in the bathroom and press my back against the door. This is just…*crazy.*

Is this how Kane feels when he's in the middle of one of his glass shows and hundreds of people come to see him?

Kane's so moody, so *grouchy*, I can't imagine that going over well with him.

Then again, he's loosened up considerably since he met Anastasia.

It doesn't take me too long to buff and polish myself in the shower since I'm not washing my hair. I slip into my strapless bra and panties that I brought just for this occasion and wrap myself in a thick, luxurious cashmere robe before walking back out to be transformed into a woman worthy of being on Hunter's arm on the red carpet.

"I DO BELIEVE our work here is finished."

Three hours. It took three freaking hours to finish said *work*. I'm used to taking thirty minutes to slap on a little makeup and do something with my hair.

This was another experience altogether.

I have lashes. Not the kind you glue onto your eyelid. No, these have been added to my *actual* lashes. They should last several weeks, and if I choose to, I can start seeing someone to keep them filled in all the time.

We decided to leave my hair down because it's thick, and if we did an up-do, there was concern that it would either look bridal or like I was going to the prom.

So, for several hours, someone stood behind me with a curling iron and carefully sculpted every strand.

I've just stepped into my dress and am itching to look in the nearby full-length mirror.

"Can I look now?" I ask.

"Don't worry," I'm assured, "we have smelling salts for when you faint. Just don't mess up your hair."

I laugh and walk over to the mirror. And then I just stand and stare.

"Is that *me*?"

"It's all you. We just enhanced you."

"Everyone out."

It's Hunter's voice. There's a bit of commotion around me, and then the door closes.

The air is charged.

I slowly turn around and see that Hunter, who was already the sexiest man alive, is wearing a black tux. What is it about muscled men in tuxes? It fits him like a damn glove.

It makes a girl salivate.

"I—"

He doesn't finish the sentence, he just stares, unblinking, taking me in from head to toe the way he did the first time he saw me.

"You look nice," I say lamely, suddenly feeling uncomfortable.

"I've swallowed my tongue," he says at last and rubs his fingers over his lips. "For fuck's sake, we can't go tonight."

"Why? Is this not appropriate?"

"I'll kill them all." I blink at him, and my stomach loosens a bit. "They'll stare at you, *want* you, and I'll have to murder them."

"I think you're safe from that." I laugh and step to him, straightening his tie. "I'm glad you like it."

"I don't think I just like it." He swallows hard. "What I'm feeling can't be that simple."

"It's just a dress. And a super special necklace."

"It's the woman in them." He grins. "I want to kiss you, but I don't want to mess you up."

"They left the tube of lipstick for me."

The kiss is gentle. It always surprises me how tender he is with me given how strong and big he is.

Finally, he pulls back and sighs.

"We have to go. I have to share you with the world for a while. And then, I have some special things planned for later."

"Good God, Hunter, I can't take any more special plans. I'll die of a heart attack."

He laughs and passes me my clutch.

When we walk into the hallway, I'm surprised to see two men, two *huge* men, waiting for us.

I turn to Hunter and raise a brow.

"This is Sid and Harry. They're our bodyguards for the night."

"Wait, what? Why in the world do we need bodyguards?"

"Because Mr. Meyers is a very famous man. One who receives threats." Sid nods, and we walk toward the elevator.

"But, why?"

"Because I beat people up for a living, babe." Hunter winks at me. "And while I have no problem protecting myself, I won't risk anything happening to you."

I swallow hard and will the tears away.

I will *not* ruin this makeup masterpiece.

But I'm pretty sure I just finished falling head over heels in love with this man.

Once in the limo, I glance at Sid and Harry and then at Hunter.

"You can say anything," Hunter assures me. "They've signed NDAs."

"I'm just curious. I meant to say something on the plane but was distracted." I grin. "If I'm the first woman you've brought to something like this, aren't you worried about what the press will say?"

"Do I seem like the kind of man who worries about the press?"

"No." I laugh but then shrug. "But they'll ask questions. What will you say when they ask you who I am?"

He takes my hand and kisses my fingers. "I'll tell them the truth. That you're someone who means a lot to me, and that I'm grateful you agreed to accompany me this evening. That's all they need to know, Maeve. What happens between you and me is *our* business. Now, we're almost there. We'll walk the red carpet. Don't worry, I'll coach you through it."

"Oh, no big deal. Just the red carpet."

Sid's lips twitch with humor.

"All you have to do is smile. I'll be with you the whole time, of course."

"So, you're nominated tonight," I say, needing to talk to keep my nerves somewhat calm. "What else are you doing? Are you presenting?"

"I'm presenting the Kobe Bryant Lifetime Achievement Award," he says. "So, I spent some time while you were getting ready going over the speech. And I thought I should put together some words just in case I win something."

"It surprises me that you're nominated, given you're retired."

"I've only been retired for about four months," he says. "So, I was still eligible for this year's nominations."

"You'll win." I squeeze his hand. "Now that you *are* retired, are you going to miss all of this?"

"More than you'll ever know." He glances out the window of the limo.

"Then why retire?"

"That's a conversation for another time." He kisses my hand once more as the car comes to a stop. Sid and Harry climb out first, and it's just a sea of flashing bulbs and lights and so many *people.*

Hunter exits the car, much to the crowd's delight. He nods, then turns back for me, extending his hand as he helps me up.

We pause and wait as flashbulbs go off and people gather around to take our photo, and then we're ushered onto the red carpet to make way for the next limo.

"We just stop on the black marks," Hunter whispers in my ear.

The red carpet looks so glamorous on TV. But it's just a long stretch of carpet with ropes along the front so the photographers and interviewers can't get too close. We stop every twenty feet or so to pose, smile, and answer a couple of questions.

When we get to an ESPN reporter that I recognize, Hunter leads me to him and smiles at the other man.

"Hey, man," Hunter says and shakes his hand. "It's good to see you."

"You're looking dapper as always," the other guy says. I can't remember his name. Alan? Kevin? "And who is this?"

"This is my date, Maeve O'Callaghan," Hunter says, introducing me. "Maeve, this is Stephen A. Smith."

"Nice to meet you," I reply and suddenly have a microphone in my face.

What in the hell do I do now?

"Maeve O'Callaghan," Stephen A. says with a grin. "I do believe you're the first date I've seen with this guy."

I simply smile back at him.

"How do you know each other?"

I glance at Hunter who just grins down at me.

"I sold him a house," I say simply. "It's not a terribly exciting story."

We're being cued to move on, so Stephen A. says his goodbyes, and then we're ushered into an auditorium.

We're seated in the front row.

Next to Vanessa Bryant.

Kobe's widow is absolutely stunning in a white dress and diamonds that sparkle almost as brightly as the bulbs that flashed on the carpet.

She's seated on the other side of Hunter, and they say hello to each other before she smiles at me. She's so welcoming; I'm taken off guard.

"Just flag me down if you need help," she assures me. "For the most part, it's boring. But I'll be here when Hunter has to go do his thing."

"Thank you so much," I say with a smile.

"I have to go say hello to someone," Hunter says and kisses me on the cheek. "I'll be right back."

"O'Callaghan. I love that name," Vanessa continues. "You're not, by any chance, related to Kane O'Callaghan, are you?"

"He's my brother," I confirm with a proud smile.

"Oh, that's so great. I have several of his pieces in my home. What do you do, Maeve?"

"I sell real estate and help out in our family-owned pub. It's not terribly glamorous, but it's a lot of fun."

She leans over as if she's about to tell me a secret. "Glamorous is overrated. *Fun* matters. Also, before he comes back, I just have to tell you that you and Hunter make a gorgeous couple."

"Thanks." I glance over to where Hunter is chatting with a man I recognize and then realize it's a football player. And not just any player. Will Montgomery. "Oh, gosh. Will's here! I'm so sorry, Vanessa, please excuse me."

"Of course."

I hurry over to the two men and grin when Will sees me.

"You're here," I say with excitement and am swept up in a big hug. "Where's Meg?"

"In the bathroom. I wish they'd serve food at these things."

I laugh and shake my head. Will is known as being the food lover of the family. He's *always* hungry.

"I didn't realize that you two knew each other," Will says and raises an eyebrow at my date.

"We haven't known each other long," I reply and slip my hand into Hunter's. "I thought for sure it would have made its way through the family gossip line by now because Jules and Nat helped me pick out this dress."

"No one tells me anything," Will says and grins when his wife joins him.

"Oh my God, Maeve," Meg says and reaches out to hug me. "Holy shit, the girls were right. You're stunning in this dress."

"You knew?" Will demands.

"Yeah, and I *told* you. Twice. But you never listen to me."

The lights dim, and Hunter squeezes my hand.

"We'd better grab our seats."

"Will we see you at the after-party?" Meg asks.

"No," Hunter says before I can reply. "We have other plans."

"Girls' night," I remind Meg as we start to walk away. "As soon as possible."

"I'm so there, girl."

We make our way back to our seats, and I'm surprised to discover that a lot of what happens at awards shows is waiting. For commercials, for things to get set up. But it's also fascinating and so much more exciting in person.

Will Montgomery, to my absolute shock, is hosting the show. I glance back at Meg, who just grins at me and sits back to enjoy Will's fun banter and jokes. He's handsome and funny, and perfect for the show.

"I have to go backstage," Hunter whispers to me. "I'm presenting the next award."

"Okay. Good luck."

He kisses my cheek, and then he's gone. Ten minutes later, he's onstage to present the Kobe Bryant Lifetime Achievement Award.

Hunter is an amazingly good public speaker. He's poised, his voice is clear, and he doesn't seem to be nervous at all.

And when all is said and done, and he returns to his seat, Vanessa gives Hunter a long, tight hug.

"Thank you," she murmurs to him.

"It's my absolute honor," Hunter replies.

Soon, the category of fighter of the year is introduced. I clasp Hunter's hand and hold my breath until they announce *Hunter Meyers* as the winner.

He glances down at me, grins, and kisses me square on the mouth for the cameras to see before walking up on stage to accept the award.

"Thank you," he says. "This means more than you know."

He keeps it that simple and is escorted off the stage.

Another hour goes by before the last award of the evening, athlete of the year, is introduced.

Again, I take his hand and hold my breath.

"And the ESPY goes to…Hunter Meyers."

Hunter looks genuinely surprised this time when he looks down at me, kisses me once more, and then climbs the steps of the stage to accept his award.

"I honestly wasn't expecting this," he admits when the applause dies down. "You know, I made the decision last year to retire from MMA because I have a daughter who needs me. I love this industry. It's been a part of who I am for more than twenty years. But Rachel *is* my heart, so I have to thank her first for putting up with me. My parents are the best people in the world, and I couldn't have had the career I did without their help and support."

He swallows hard and then looks down at me. What in the world could he thank me for? I didn't even know him when he was fighting.

"I'm starting a new chapter in my life, and sometimes new chapters can be scary. Even for brawlers like me. But there's a woman with me tonight that has shifted my world for the better."

He winks at me, and I grin back at him.

"Thank you, everyone, for this honor."

He nods and is then escorted off the stage.

"Wow," Vanessa says and grins at me. "Congratulations."

"Thank you."

The camera is still on me, so I just clap and smile, wishing we were already alone.

CHAPTER 10

~MAEVE~

When we finally make our way back to the suite, I'm exhausted. Despite Hunter's plans to skip out on the parties, we still had to stay and talk to people, and the press followed us, yelling questions all the way to the car.

"I knew they'd jump on this story," I say after I walk into the room and set my clutch on a table. "It's juicy gossip."

"They'll find something else to talk about tomorrow," he says and loosens his tie.

Both of his trophies were delivered to the hotel and sit on the dining room table.

"Congratulations," I say as I cross to him. "I was super proud of you tonight."

"Thank you." He drags his fingertips down my cheek. "That last one was a surprise."

"I could tell. But you deserve it."

He grins. "Have you ever actually sat down to watch one of my fights, babe?"

"Well, no." I cringe. "Sorry. I didn't know you then, and I can't say it was really my jam. But Keegan always had your fights playing in the pub. So, technically, I did see your work."

He chuckles, but before he can say anything, the doorbell rings.

"I don't know about you," he says as he crosses to the door, "but I'm starving."

"Oh God, yes. The charcuterie spread from earlier is long gone."

A waiter pushes a table on wheels into the room. "Would you like me to dress the dining table, sir?"

"No, thanks. This is fine." Hunter tips the man, who nods stiffly.

"Very well, sir. Have a good evening."

"What do we have?" I ask as I cross to the table. "Please tell me it's stuff I won't spill on this dress. I would change, but I was told to let you peel it off me, so I'm holding out."

He blinks, surprised, and then re-covers the plate with the silver dome and moves to me.

"Let's get comfortable," he suggests and wraps his arms around me. Without looking, he drags the zipper down my back and lets the gown fall around my ankles. "Fucking hell, that's all you've had on under there this whole time?"

"The crew made me lose the bra," I say with a shrug. "They said the dress was better without it."

I'm standing before him in just a scrap of black lace panties, the emerald hanging almost to my breasts, and black heels.

Hunter simply lifts me, and without another word, carries me to the bedroom.

"What about our food?" I ask with a laugh.

"It'll be there when we're done." He doesn't lower me to the bed as I expected him to. Instead, he just sets me on my feet, steps back, and takes me in. "You're every damn fantasy come to life."

"Come here." I crook a finger at him and laugh when he just raises an eyebrow. "Please."

His movements are slow and measured as he stalks toward me. When he's mere inches away, I glide my hands up his chest and get to work unbuttoning his shirt.

"I enjoyed spending a few hours in your world," I tell him softly. "You're clearly well-respected and liked by all of the people in that room. Even the fighters you've beaten in the past had a smile for you. It tells me some things."

I guide the shirt over his broad shoulders and down his arms, letting it fall to the floor.

"You *do* have some tattoos." I can't mask the surprise in my voice.

"I didn't want too much ink," he says as I trace the lion on his upper arm. "What were you going to say?"

"That I was right about you all along. You're an alpha male for sure. You like to take care of people. You like to take charge. But you're also kind and a good person. Anyone who meets Rachel would know that because those are the values you've already instilled in her."

I dip my fingertip into his slacks as Hunter cups my cheek and rubs his thumb over the apple of it.

"But what I knew, first and foremost, the minute I first saw you, is that you're sexier than any one man has a right to be. And I've wanted to get you like this for weeks now."

His jaw clenches, and his eyes narrow. He moves in, kissing me like a man starved as he urges me back until my legs hit the side of the bed.

He lifts me easily and lays me on the cool linens. His mouth immediately latches on to my breast, and his fingers start to roam.

"No fair," I say, my breath already coming fast. "I wasn't finished undressing you."

"If you think I can keep my hands off you for even one more minute, you're crazy."

His mouth, his hands, are *everywhere,* seemingly all at once. My body heats under his intense attention.

His arms and back are all smooth skin and rigid muscle, and I can't stop touching him. I slip my hands into his pants and cup his bare ass.

"Naked," I say firmly. "Get fucking naked, Hunter."

He smiles against my skin and then hurries off the

bed to stand before me. I brace myself on my elbows and watch as he shucks his shoes, socks, and *finally*, his pants.

He's impressively aroused.

And a piece of metal catches the light.

"Uh, Hunter?"

I scoot to the edge of the bed to get a better look.

"Yeah."

"You're pierced."

"I am."

With just my fingertip, I touch the little ball of silver at the top of his cock, and he groans.

Suddenly, I'm on my back once more, and Hunter is kissing my neck while his hands roam all over me.

"You're *pierced.*"

He chuckles. "Yes."

"Why?"

He leans up to look down at me. "A few of us got them when I was young. I just kept it."

Stunned, I cup his face, push his shoulder, and smile when he rolls onto his back, reversing our positions.

"I need to check this out."

I kiss and lick my way down his torso, over abs that could be sculpted from marble, and kiss the very tip of him, right next to the metal.

"Fucking hell."

He covers his face with his arm, his hands clenched.

I settle in to work him over. To make him as crazy as he made me on the plane earlier today.

Was that just *today?*

So much has happened since then, it feels like days ago.

His dick is warm, smooth, and hard as hell as I lick and suck him.

"Enough."

He rears up, grabs my shoulders, and reverses our position again, pinning my hands above my head as he stares down at me, breathing hard.

"Fucking hell, you can't just do that and expect me to keep my shit together." He nips at my bottom lip. "I'm too damn hot for you."

"That doesn't hurt my feelings at all." I push against his hands and *love* how strong he is. That he's not even trying hard, and I'm totally at his will. "I have birth control covered."

His eyes flare. "Are you sure? I'll suit up."

I just shake my head slowly, and with his eyes pinned to mine, I raise my legs high on his hips, feeling the tip of him nudge me.

He clenches his eyes shut for just a second.

"God, it's gonna be snug."

I bite my lip, and he gently pushes inside of me. I can feel those tiny metal balls gliding over my walls, and it's unlike anything I've ever felt before.

And when he's fully seated, he tips his forehead against mine, lets my arms go, and kisses me tenderly.

"Holy shit, Hunter."

"Is that a good holy shit?"

"So good." I gasp when he starts to move. "Jesus, who knew a little piece of metal could do so much?"

His grin is cocky as he picks up the pace. He keeps hitting just the right spot that sends shivers right through me, shooting electricity up my spine.

I clench around him. My toes curl, and every muscle in my body tightens as the climax moves through me.

"Shit," he whispers. "Oh, God."

He pushes once more and then pulses as he empties himself into me.

"Holy shit," I murmur when my lips are no longer numb. My stomach growls, making us both laugh. "If I wasn't hungry before, I'm starving now."

He cups my face and kisses me softly, in that gentle way he does that makes the butterflies in my stomach sit up and take notice. He nibbles the side of my mouth, then nuzzles my nose.

"You're amazing," he whispers. "You do things to me that I never knew were possible."

I sigh softly and rest my forehead against his. "Same goes, Mr. Meyers." I kiss his chin. "Can we eat now?"

He grins as I slide off the bed and reach for his discarded shirt. I pull it on, rolling the sleeves, and buttoning just a couple of the fasteners.

"You think that shirt will keep you safe from me?" he asks.

"I hope not."

~

IT'S EARLY when I wake up with Hunter snoring peacefully next to me. Dawn is barely starting to fill the sky above Los Angeles.

I check the time. It's just past five.

Doesn't surprise me.

I don't sleep much. I never have. And with my crazy hours at the pub, it's a good thing I don't require a ton of sleep.

I don't want to wake Hunter, so I slip out of the bed, grab some leggings and a T-shirt that I brought with me, and pile my laptop and phone in my arms as I sneak out of the bedroom soundlessly.

It's too early to wake him. We had a busy night. Not just with the ESPYs, but also with several hours of sex afterward.

The man is almost superhuman.

I grin as I pull the T-shirt over my head and tug on the leggings. Before I open my computer and get to work, I order up some room service but ask them to knock lightly and not ring the bell.

My body hurts in places I forgot I had. Muscles are sore, joints tender.

Yes, we had fun last night.

I set my laptop on the end of the dining room table. In fact, this is a lovely workspace with the same gorgeous view as the bedroom and plenty of space to spread out.

I've just opened my computer when there's a light knock on the door.

I smile at the waitress as she walks in carrying a large tray full of coffee, fruit, and pastries.

"On the dining table is perfect," I instruct her and stand back as she unloads everything onto the table, then tucks the tray under her arm and passes me the bill.

I sign my name, add a tip, and escort her out.

I need coffee.

I pour myself a cup, doctor it up the way I like it, and take a bite of a decadent cinnamon roll as I sit in front of the computer.

With everything that's happened over the past few days, the catastrophe at my house, and taking this trip, I'm behind on some work. This is the perfect opportunity to get caught up before we make our way back to Seattle.

I open my email and start with the oldest first. This one, Dale Rimmon, is a client that I've corresponded with, but haven't met in person.

His emails usually raise red flags. I can't even put a finger on why, he just makes me uncomfortable.

Dear Maeve,

I will be in town for a few days in a few weeks. I would like to see several homes at that time. As I narrow down my exact dates, I'll be in touch. I will want to see you, and only you.

Sincerely,

Dale

I take a deep breath. "Jesus, Dale, could you be any creepier? Why me and only me?"

I shake my head. Maybe he's just not good with email.

I answer several other emails and do some property research per several clients' requests. Just as I'm about to finish up for the morning, Hunter comes rushing out of the bedroom, haphazardly dressed and barking into his cell phone.

"I don't know where she is. We need to find her."

He stops short and stares at me.

I stare back.

"Never mind. I found her."

He clicks off and just drops his phone onto the couch.

"Hi." I raise a brow.

"Jesus, I thought you left." He scrubs his hand over his face.

I look around the room and then back at Hunter. "Where would I go? I'm with you. It's a big suite, Hunter. I had work and didn't want to wake you."

"Just wake me." He walks over and kisses the top of my head. "It gave me a bad moment."

My hand covers his on my shoulder. "Okay, now I know. I have coffee and some sugar here if you want some."

"I'll order up a protein shake."

I smile up at him. "That does not sound like a delightful breakfast."

"It's just fuel," he says. "How long have you been up?"

"Just over an hour. I don't sleep much."

"Was I snoring?"

I laugh and stand so I can wrap my arms around him for a hug. "No. Okay, maybe a little, but you didn't wake me. I'm just not much of a sleeper. It's not unusual for me to only get a few hours a night and then get up and do stuff."

"I'll remember that."

His finger dips into the neckline of my shirt and he tugs out the emerald.

"You're still wearing it."

"I like it."

"I'm glad."

"Who did you call? When you thought I was gone?"

"Sid," he says.

"And how would Sid be able to track me down?"

"He's former CIA," he replies simply.

"Of course, he is."

"WHAT DO you mean it's going to take *two months* to fix my house?" I demand and prop my hands on my hips. Hunter and I have been back in town for two hours. He and Rachel are settling in at his place, and I had to meet with the contractor who's taking care of my home.

"It's my busiest time of year," Grant says, shaking his head mournfully. "And this isn't going to be a quick job. The house is damn old, Maeve. Looks like no one replaced the roof in more than twenty years. And you have some internal structural damage going on. I'm not sure what it's from. It could just be old-fashioned rot because the house is—"

"Damn old," I finish for him. "Can I live in it?"

Grant frowns. "We get more rain, I can't guarantee you won't get wet. And, I'll be honest, it's always easier if you're not underfoot. You have lots of family here. I'm sure there's somewhere you can go for a while."

"Yeah." I chew my lip and stare at my little white house. "I have places to go, but it's never as good as home."

"Listen, I'll try to get to it sooner. My advice is, get most of the stuff out of here and into storage so nothing else gets ruined, and then let us work our magic. I'll be in touch."

"Yeah, okay. Thanks, Grant."

Grant nods, gets in his big work truck, and drives away.

The estimate for what it's going to cost to fix keeps bouncing around in my head. It's a big chunk of money. It'll take up at least half of my savings.

But this is what it costs to be a homeowner.

It's not always flowerbeds and picking out paint

swatches.

I wonder if Hunter will be okay with me staying in his garage apartment for a couple of months. He seems to be perfectly fine with having me around, but sixty days or more is a lot to ask. Especially given that our relationship is so new. And Grant was right, I *do* have plenty of family here that I could stay with.

Hell, Maggie has space in her house.

I drive the short distance to Mary Margaret's and knock on her door.

"You just caught me," she says when she opens it. "I was about to head to the pub."

"I'll be there in a few hours," I tell her and follow her to the kitchen. I tell her all about my meeting with Grant. "It's going to take a lot of time to fix it, and I might need a place to stay."

"I have space."

"I know. I think it's best if I move in here. I don't want to wear out my welcome with Hunter, you know? Things are still so new."

"I get it. It's not a problem. Do you need help moving your stuff?"

"Nah, I can manage. Thanks. I'm going to head over there and start packing. I'll probably move in here tomorrow."

"Sounds good. All I ask is that if you and Hunter decide to do the dirty, don't do it when I'm home."

"I think we can manage to keep ourselves under control."

CHAPTER 11

~HUNTER~

"It was so cool," Rachel says as she unpacks her overnight bag. She's been talking nonstop since we arrived back on the island, and Maeve went to check on her house. "Grams and Gramps and I watched every minute of it. Maeve was *so* pretty. And then you won, and we were yelling and screaming and jumping up and down. And you even said my name in your speech."

"What other name would I say?"

She rolls her eyes, making me grin.

"And it was sweet, what you said at the end about the new chapter and meeting someone new."

"You know, now that you say that, I'd like to have a chat with you. Let's go sit out here."

I turn and walk to the lounge area that Rachel and I made in the loft space. We have a big TV, leather couches, and a ping-pong table with room to spare.

"What's wrong? Did it go bad? Are you breaking up with her?"

"Good God, you have an active imagination," I mutter and sit across from my daughter. "No, it didn't go badly at all. In fact, we had a great time."

Rachel deflates in relief.

She's a bit dramatic.

"You're not a baby anymore, and I'm not going to insult either of us by thinking that you're not an intelligent young woman who knows what goes on between two people who care about each other."

"Sex." The word is simple, and matter of fact, and puts a lump in my stomach.

"Among other things. Also, side note, if you start having sex, I want you to tell me. I'm serious. I need to make sure you're safe."

"I'm not," she says and rolls her eyes again. "Boys are scared of me because you're my dad."

I grin. "Really? That's great."

Rachel narrows her eyes.

"I mean, how horrible for you. Anyway, I care about Maeve, Rach."

"You love her." She smiles and reaches over to pat my shoulder. "You just don't know it yet."

You're wrong. I know it.

"I want to move forward with her and see if this is something that might stick for the long haul. And I don't want her to stay in that apartment."

Rachel frowns. "Then where would she…? *Oh.* You want her to sleep with *you*."

"I do, but only if it doesn't freak you out. Because as you know, you're the most important part of my life, and I don't bring women home. You know that."

"I know. That's how I know she's really important to you. And I like her, Dad. I like her whole family. They're really cool."

"They're definitely cool," I agree. "I don't want you to feel disrespected if I ask her to move in with me."

Rachel licks her lips and thinks it over. "Grams said something last night that I hadn't thought of before. And it's true. She said that in just a few years, I'll be off to college, living my own life, and you'll be moving onto another new part of life. An *empty nester* or what-ever. And that it's okay for you to start thinking about yourself more. I wasn't complaining or anything. She was just talking. Dad, it's okay. I like Maeve, and I know that nothing's going to change between you and me."

"If something makes you uncomfortable, I want you to say so," I reply, my heart in my throat. "Because even though you're going to leave me when you're thirty, I still love you more than anything."

"Uh, I'm leaving before I'm thirty."

"Twenty-eight then."

She laughs. "Sure, Dad. Ask her to move in. Just *please* don't do anything gross when I'm around. Because that's just…ew."

"It's a deal." I pull her over so I can kiss her on the cheek and ruffle her hair. "We need to start planning for school."

"It doesn't start for, like, two months," she says.

"It's a new school. I want to be prepared for it."

"I need clothes," she says, thinking it over. "And all new supplies. Maybe Maeve will take me shopping."

And just like that, I'm no longer the cool one.

"What am I, chopped liver?"

"You can come, too, I guess, since you're the one paying."

"Come back here, you little shit," I call when she runs away, laughing. "Yeah, you'd better hide!"

"You don't scare me!"

I laugh, relieved that the discussion went better than expected, and walk down to the kitchen. I glance out the window and scowl.

Maeve is hauling stuff out to her car, and the luggage is heavy given the way she has to lug it up into her vehicle.

"What's up?" I ask as I walk out the door and join her by her car.

"Oh, I'm just taking a few things over to Maggie's."

"You're taking your suitcase over to your sister's?"

"Yeah." She clears her throat. "I was going to talk to you, but then I got carried away upstairs. I met with the contractor, and he said it's going to be at least two months before my house is done. And we all know that means three months. That's a long time to inconvenience you, so I spoke with Maggie, and she said I can just stay with her."

"Let's go inside." I turn toward the door and open it for her, then follow her into the kitchen. "Have I somehow given you the impression that having you here is an inconvenience?"

She frowns. "Well, no. Of course, not, I just thought that because this thing between us is so new, that it was inappropriate to assume that I could just stay for as long as I like."

"This *thing*." I cross my arms and watch her from across the island. I want to pull her against me and crush my mouth to hers. I want to remind her that this isn't just a *thing*.

"Why are you mad?"

"Because you made a decision that involves me without talking with me." I rub my fingers over my lips. "I don't want you to go."

"Oh. Well, okay. I can stay above the garage—"

"I also don't want you to stay out there."

She frowns again and blinks at me. "Then where in the world will I stay?"

"With me."

Silence.

"*With* me."

"We've already said that it's not right for me to stay with you with Rachel here."

"Rachel and I talked about it. She's not stupid, she understands what's going on with us. This *thing*. And she likes you. Not to mention, she wants to see me happy. So, she and I are on the same page and understand each other."

"Why are you so frustrated?" she asks again.

"Because I've been planning a way to keep you with me, *really* with me, not out in my guest house, and you've been scheming up a way to escape. I thought we had a good time in LA."

"We did."

"I thought that we'd taken this *thing* to a whole new level."

"You don't like that I called us a *thing*."

"No. I don't. Because, damn it, I'm falling in love with you. And you've made how I feel into something small and insignificant."

She shakes her head, those green eyes bright.

"No, this is a lot of miscommunication—which I hate because we're adults, and miscommunication is for bad romantic comedies." She walks around the island and takes my hands, moving them around her waist to her lower back, and then leans into me. "I'm not trying to run. I just didn't want to assume. This is new territory for me, you know?"

"Yeah." I sigh and tip my forehead against hers. "And I'm an asshole. I don't want you to go to Maggie's."

"I gathered as much. And it's pleased I am that you had a talk with your daughter."

"Your Irish is coming out." The way it does when she's turned on.

"I'm all worked up," she admits. "First it was the bloody contractor. And then trying to decide what to do from there. Are you sure you want me here, underfoot, for several months?"

Forever.

The word almost slips out of my mouth, but I catch it.

"You are welcome here indefinitely."

She smiles and lifts on tiptoe to kiss my lips. "Thank you."

"Child entering," Rachel calls out. "In case there's anything goofy going on in there."

Maeve laughs and steps away from me. "Nothing goofy."

"So, are you staying?" Rachel asks.

"Looks like it. Were you eavesdropping?" I ask my daughter.

"Of course, I was," Rachel says. "Don't worry, I won't make a habit of it."

"I have to take my bags back upstairs." Maeve walks toward the door. "No, wait. I need to bring them in *here*. Sorry, habit."

"Why don't we help Maeve move her things, and then we'll all go out to dinner?" I ask Rachel.

"I would love to, but I have to work," Maeve says. "I'm expected at the pub in just a bit. But you're welcome to come and eat there."

"I totally want some of Fiona's stew," Rachel says. "I told Gramps about it, and he said that he and

Grams will come see us next weekend. He wants stew, too."

"It's the best there is," Maeve agrees.

We spend an hour moving her things from the vehicle and apartment to the house, and then Maeve comes out of the bedroom dressed in her O'Callaghan's Pub shirt and denim shorts.

"Have I told you that your legs are fucking amazing?" I ask her as I wrap my arms around her waist.

"No, you haven't. But thanks. I find if I wear shorts, I get better tips."

I narrow my eyes. "You're kidding."

"I certainly am not." She grins and pats my cheek. "I have a roof to pay for. Why are roofs so damn expensive anyway?"

"Maeve—"

"No." Her smile fades, and she's perfectly serious now. "You're not going to pay for my roof, Hunter. I can afford it. I'm just mostly kidding about the tips."

"You're not kidding." I wish she'd just let me pay for it. It's *nothing* to me. And here she is, working her ass off to afford it.

"Okay, I'm not totally joking. But if all it takes to get an extra five bucks is to wear a pair of shorts, who cares?"

"Maybe I care."

She laughs. "Right. You have no reason to. Besides, you're the man who used to be on national television in your underwear."

"It was *inter*national television, thank you very much."

She barks out a laugh, and I join her. "See? They're just shorts. No one gets to touch my legs but you."

"Damn right."

"YOU HAVE A BABY IN A BAR," Maeve says to Izzy when we walk into the pub. Izzy's rocking the baby back and forth, but the sweet thing won't stop crying.

"She has colic," Izzy says. She looks exhausted. "Sometimes, if Keegan rocks her, she'll stop crying. But he's swamped, and I'm exhausted."

"I've got her," I say and step forward, my arms outstretched for the infant. "Rachel had colic, too, and I was a single dad. I get it. Has she eaten?"

"About an hour ago," Izzy confirms.

"Go catch a nap," I reply as I set the baby on my shoulder and pat her tiny back. "I've got this."

"Are you sure?" But the hope in Izzy's eyes is unmistakable.

"Go," Maeve says. "If we need anything, we'll come up."

"I'm not going to cry," Izzy says as she turns away and flees up the stairs.

I tuck the blanket around the baby more firmly and hold her close. "There now, sugar. Aren't you tired from making all that racket?"

She quiets and takes a big, deep breath.

"That's right. You just needed someone calm, didn't you?"

I kiss the baby's soft head and then glance up to find Maeve, Maggie, Rachel, and Fiona all staring at me in surprise.

"What?"

"Well, if I've ever seen anything sweeter in all of my life, I couldn't say what it was," Fiona says as a smile spreads over her face. "You're so good with her."

"I like babies." I kiss her head again. "What's her name?"

"They haven't named her yet," Maggie says. "They can't agree on the name, so for now, we're just calling her Baby."

"I don't mind calling you Baby, if you don't," I say to the little infant in my arms.

Maeve wraps her apron around her waist, and Rachel sits next to me at the bar, sipping on a root beer.

"You look good with a babe on your shoulder," Keegan says when he walks behind the bar. "Did my wife flee then?"

"I told her to go get some sleep," I reply with a smile. "I have experience with cranky babies. And cranky teenagers, now that I think about it."

"Hey," Rachel says in protest, making me laugh. "I'm not *always* cranky."

"Only on days that end in *y*," I agree, and she sticks out her tongue at me, then turns to Keegan.

"Mr. O'Callaghan, are you hiring?"

I blink at my daughter. "What?"

"Well, I might be. What kind of job are you after, lass?"

"I'd do just about anything. I can waitress or clean up. Buss tables. That sort of thing. School starts in a month, but I'd still be able to work on the weekends."

I stare at her, stunned. I had no idea that she wanted a job, but it's a good idea.

"You can't serve alcohol as you're underage," Keegan tells her. "So, you can't be a server. But you could help seat the customers when they arrive and run food out from the kitchen. Buss those tables and wipe them off. And I can always use someone to help me wash the glasses back here."

Rachel sits forward with excitement. "I would be happy to do all of those things."

Keegan nods as though he's thinking it over. "Would you be able to start tomorrow afternoon then?"

"Yes!" Rachel claps her hands and smiles over at me. "I just got a job, Dad!"

"So you did. That's good. You can start paying rent."

"Har har." Rachel sips her drink happily.

"I'll have Maeve get you a couple of T-shirts as that's our uniform around here. But we're casual, so jeans are just fine to go with it."

"Come on," Maeve says and motions for Rachel to follow her. "Let's go pick out a couple. We have a new pink one that'll look great on you."

The two of them head back to the storeroom, and I shift the baby to my other shoulder.

"Thanks for that."

"Rachel's a good lass. She's happy and helpful, and I think it'll be good for her. She might meet some new people, too, because we get plenty of locals who come in for the food."

"That's a great idea. I didn't even think of it, and I should have."

The baby starts to fuss, so I stand and walk her around the pub crooning in her ear.

It feels good to hold a little baby again. Rachel grew up in the blink of an eye, and I missed a good portion of it because I was always gone.

I never considered having more kids, but I didn't have Maeve in my life before this either.

Just as I think that, the woman comes back into the bar area with my daughter. When her eyes meet mine, she grins widely.

Maybe this new chapter is more interesting than I originally thought.

CHAPTER 12

~MAEVE~

"It was so nice of your mother to give us this tub of stew," Angie Meyers says. Hunter's parents have been in town for three days, and the five of us are gathered in Hunter's home, enjoying Sunday brunch before Angie and Jay head back to Seattle. "I'm going to freeze some of it so it lasts us a while."

"We're not that far away," Hunter reminds his mom and kisses her head before setting a platter of bacon on the table. "You two can come over anytime, stay in the guest house. Eat stew."

"We might do that," Jay says, looking up from his newspaper. "In fact, your mother and I were talking last night. We were going to wait to mention it. Give it some more thought."

"Let's just tell them," Angie says with excitement and reaches over for Rachel's hand.

"We'd like to move to the island," Jay says. "Of

course, we need to sell the house in Seattle and look for something here, but we want to be close to you. You're our family."

I glance over at Hunter and see a smile spread across his handsome face—one so much like his father's.

"That might be the best news I've heard in a *very* long time," Hunter says. "I didn't want to pressure you guys to come here, especially because it was my decision to move out of the city. And I know you like it there."

"Well, it's just a ferry ride away," Angie reminds her son. "We love it here. The views are gorgeous, and we enjoyed Maeve's family very much. And being close to you is important to us."

Hunter and I share a look. He was hoping that having them here this weekend would have this exact result.

"Well," he says with a nod and takes a bite of bacon, "I know an excellent realtor."

"I was hoping to talk to you about this," Angie says to me. "Give you an idea of what we might be looking for and see if there's anything available."

"I have quite a lot for sale right now," I reply. "What are you thinking?"

Rachel is all smiles as we discuss what Jay and Angie would like in a new home. They want charm, not *too* much space, a pretty view, and to be nearby in case Rachel needs them.

"I'll start doing some digging tonight after we get back from Seattle," I assure them. "Speaking of that, we should probably get ready to go."

"I'm stuffed," Jay says. "I'll help with dishes."

"Oh, you don't have to do that," I assure him, but he shakes his head and stands to clear the table.

"That's his way of saying he'd like a moment alone with you," Angie says with a wink and carries her plate to the sink. "I'll just go out to the guest house and make sure we've got everything."

I glance around, suddenly realizing I'm alone with Jay, who's busy rinsing dishes and loading them into the dishwasher.

He's a tall man with silver threaded through his dark hair. He's in excellent physical shape, just like his son.

I set the leftover juice in the fridge, put lids on the fruit bowls, and stow them away as well.

We work in companionable silence for at least five minutes.

"We like you," he says at last, catching my attention. "One of the reasons we came this weekend was to get to know you a bit, to see how you are with Rachel and our boy."

Jay smiles kindly and wipes his wet hands with a towel.

"And, of course, to see their new home," he adds.

"And what did you think?" I lean on the countertop and smile at him.

"The house is a slam dunk," he says. "Absolutely beautiful. You just can't beat that view."

"I couldn't agree more."

"Rachel's smiling more, coming out of her shell. She says she loved her first week of work at the pub and that she even met a couple of friends while working that she'll end up going to school with."

I nod in agreement but let him continue to talk.

"And then there's you." He tosses the sponge into the sink and turns to me. "We needed to see for ourselves how all of you fit together. To make sure that everything is…good."

"That I'm not just hanging around for your son's money?"

He doesn't immediately deny the statement. Instead, he nods slowly. "Hunter is a very wealthy man, Maeve. He's a *smart* man. And he's never been one to blindly fall in love or assume the best of everyone. In fact, we've never met anyone he's dated. We didn't even meet Rachel's mom until she was pretty far into the pregnancy.

"So, I knew that Hunter wouldn't be spending time with a woman who had ulterior motives."

"No. He wouldn't. Rachel means far too much to him. He wouldn't allow anything of the sort."

"And what does Rachel mean to *you*?" he counters.

I blow out a breath and turn to look out the window. "She's my friend," I say at last. "She makes me laugh, and I know that she cares about me. And I adore her. I enjoy working with her at the pub, and I just love the person that she is. You've all done a wonderful job of raising her to be a kind human being. Not to mention, I think my da has fallen in love with her. They put their heads together and eat my ma's cakes."

"I noticed that they've already formed a sweet bond," Jay says.

"Does that hurt you?" I ask him.

"No." He smiles and crosses his arms over his chest. "If Carla's parents were part of the picture, Rachel would have another grandfather. I don't think there's anything wrong with that girl having more people in her life who love her."

"I don't either. It's just my family's way, to include anyone we love."

His face softens. "That's the word I was looking for."

"Things are still new," I remind him. "But I wouldn't be living here while my house is fixed if I didn't love your son and Rachel. I have other places to go."

My stomach jumps at the words that just spilled from my mouth. *Love.* I love them. I'm completely in love with Hunter.

I can't imagine my life without him.

"I suspected as much. Do you think you'll be able to move out when your house is done?"

I frown. The thought of leaving them already leaves a gaping hole in my chest.

"I guess Hunter and I will cross that bridge when we come to it."

"Smart." He wraps his arm around my shoulders. "You're a smart woman, Maeve."

"I have my moments."

"Are we going shopping yet?" Rachel asks as she bounces into the kitchen. "Or is Gramps still giving you the third degree?"

"We're going shopping," I assure her. "Let's go get the others and head out."

We'll take the ferry to Seattle with Jay and Angie, and then Hunter and I plan to take Rachel shopping for school clothes and supplies. It's going to be a busy, exhausting day in the city.

"Seven pairs of jeans," Rachel says to Maggie the next afternoon at the pub. We're all working this afternoon, and Rachel is telling everyone all about our shopping trip and the loot she scored. "And way too many tops to count. Of course, new jackets because it's colder here on the island. And *tons* of shoes."

"By tons, she means three pairs," I add.

"You scored," Maggie says and offers her a high-five. "What about makeup?"

"Maeve took me into Sephora, and we picked out some things, but I don't usually wear much makeup." The door opens, and a family of four stands near the podium, waiting for a table. "Oops, that's me."

Rachel runs to seat the family, and Maggie grins at me. "She had fun."

"We all did. But let me tell you, I slept good last night. It was a *lot*. Angie and I went through Rachel's closet on Saturday to see what she already had, and we discovered that she'd outgrown most of it. So, she pretty much got a whole new wardrobe. And we're still a ways out from school starting, so she might need more."

"You know what I like?" Maggie asks as we watch Rachel smile and talk with the family she just seated. "That she's grateful. I mean, she has to know that her dad is wealthy. But she's not a spoiled brat."

"She's not," I agree. "But I will say that she also doesn't really look at price tags or worry about how much things cost. She just picks stuff out. So, while it's true that she's grateful and excited, it's also clear that she's never had to worry about a budget."

"That makes sense, though," Maggie reminds me.

"It's none of my business, but I wonder if she'll *ever* have to worry about a budget."

"She might not," Maggie says. "She's not afraid of hard work. She's shown us that much since Keegan hired her. But she may be lucky enough to work because she *likes* to, not because she has to. And there's nothing wrong with that."

I nod in agreement and then pick up my tray and make my rounds, checking in on my tables. I take a few drink refill orders and then wave at Shawn and Lexi when they walk in, ready to get started on prepping for the dinner crowd.

Since Ma and Da have been here, Ma's covered lunch. Then Shawn and Lexi take over for dinner.

I love having my parents here. When Ma's in the kitchen and Da's behind the bar, it feels like old times.

But I know they miss Ireland and will likely return there in the next couple of weeks.

Hunter pushes through the front door and blinks as his eyes adjust, then grins at me. He points to the bar and takes a seat, already chatting with Keegan.

He's started coming in every day that Rachel and I are on shift to say hello and grab a bite to eat.

We've settled into a nice little routine.

"Well, hey there, handsome." I kiss his cheek and set my tray on the bar as I turn to Keegan. "I need three Cokes, one diet, and a pitcher of water."

"How's your day so far?" Hunter asks.

"Great. It's been steady but not crazy, and everyone is happy and tipping well. We can't complain."

"Do you have a minute?" he asks.

"Sure." I flag down Maggie. "I'll be right back."

"No problem, I've got this." She winks at Hunter. "Hey there."

"Hey, back to you," he replies and walks behind me as I lead him to the storeroom.

"What's up?"

"First, this is in order." He frames my face and kisses

me, long and deep. "It's been a while since I was alone with you when we weren't both exhausted."

"We had a busy weekend," I agree with a laugh and brush my fingers through his hair. "How are you?"

"I'm great." He kisses my nose. "I got a call from my agent today. ESPN wants me to come be a guest commentator at a fight that's happening in Vegas in a few days."

"Wow, that's cool. Did you accept?"

"Well, I wanted to check with you first."

"You don't need my permission to work."

His lips twitch. "I know that. But I didn't want to leave Rachel. At least not until I talked to you about it. I can ask my parents to come over and stay with her if you'd rather. I know she'll have work, and she enjoys it here on the island. I don't want to shuttle her back and forth to the city if I don't have to. But I can if you'd rather."

"You should absolutely go. Rachel and I will be fine," I assure him. "Honest. If your parents want to come, they're welcome, but I don't think they need to. How long will you be gone?"

"Just one night. I'll leave here that morning and be back the following afternoon."

"Oh, we'll be fine," I repeat.

He leans in and kisses my forehead. "Thanks."

"We'll have ice cream and talk about boys while you're gone. You know, like girls do."

"There'd better not be any boys to talk about," he says.

I just laugh and pat him on the shoulder. "You're painfully unprepared for your daughter to have a boyfriend."

"Has someone been sniffing around her?"

"Not that I'm aware of. I'm just saying, in general. It's going to happen, Hunter. She's adorable and sweet. Some nice kid is going to be smitten."

"I'll smash his face in."

I cup his cheek. "No, you won't."

"How did we go from Vegas to my daughter having a boyfriend?"

I laugh and lead him back out to the bar. "I have to get back to work. What are you up to this afternoon?"

"I'm going to meet with some contractors. I'm having a gym built. I need more private space than I have in the house."

"You have plenty of property for it," I agree, knowing that he bought the land next to his. "That'll be great."

"What I have in mind will be better than great." He winks at me and sits back on what I've come to think of as *his* stool, and I see that one of our regulars, Freddie, is sitting next to him.

"Well, it's a fine afternoon indeed if Freddie's here." I kick up my accent a bit as Freddie's Irish himself, and I know he enjoys it. "How are you today?"

"Ah, there's a fine lass," he says with sparkling blue

eyes. "Maeve, me love, when are you going to run off and marry me?"

"As soon as I finish me shift," I assure him with a wink. "Now don't you dare go pledgin' your love to anyone else while I'm away."

Freddie takes a sip of his beer, both of us pleased as punch with our typical exchange, and I see Hunter smiling at me, clearly enjoying the show.

I take my tray of drinks and deliver them to my tables. When I glance to my right, I see a woman walk through the door and survey the room.

I don't know her, though she looks vaguely familiar.

"Um, Maeve?" Rachel asks. She slips her hand into mine, and her face has gone bone white.

"What is it? What's wrong?"

Rachel licks her lips and nods toward the woman who's now grinning and hurrying over to us.

"Uh, that's Carla. That's my mom."

"Darling!" Carla wraps her arms around Rachel, hugging her tightly. But Rachel isn't grinning. And she doesn't hug the woman back.

She only watches me with worried eyes.

"Oh, my sweet girl, it's so good to see you. Be a dear and go tell your boss you need the rest of the day off so we can catch up."

"I didn't know you were coming, Carla. I can't just take off of work."

"Since when do you call me *Carla*?" the woman

demands and then shifts her attention to me, her blue eyes icing over. "Rachel is leaving."

"No." It's Hunter's voice from behind me. "She isn't leaving."

"Well, she certainly is. *I'm* here."

"Just go," Rachel whispers. "You're embarrassing me. I'll call you when I'm finished with my shift."

"Well." Carla's face is mutinous. She brushes her hands down the red top that shows way too much cleavage. "Fine, then. I'm in town indefinitely, so I suppose there's no hurry."

I blink in surprise, and Hunter sighs as Carla spins on her heel and stalks out of the bar.

"You don't have to stay," I whisper to Rachel. "If you want to go."

"No. I have a *job*," Rachel insists. "She can't just come in here and demand that I leave."

And with that, Rachel hurries away to buss and wipe down some empty tables.

"Did you know?" I ask Hunter.

"No. But I should have." He glances down at me. "She's not here for Rachel. She's here for *you.*"

I frown. "Me? She doesn't even know me."

"She saw the ESPYs," he says. "And she's jealous. She's come to check you out and make trouble. I'm not going to Vegas. No way."

He turns away, but I tug on his arm, stopping him.

"You're going to Vegas. She's not going to mess up everything here, Hunter. She's not that important."

He just shakes his head. "We'll see how big the shit-show is by tomorrow."

He watches Rachel with worried eyes.

"Has she pulled this before?"

"No, because I've never given her a reason to. We'll talk more later. I think I'll hang around, just in case."

"Want some stew?"

"Yeah. And a beer."

CHAPTER 13

~HUNTER~

I've been sitting at the bar, brooding about the fact that Carla just waltzed in here and made a fool of herself, and decide that's a bunch of bullshit. I'm not *afraid* of her. There's absolutely nothing she can do to harm us. She signed over her rights as a mother the day after Rachel was born.

I've just always tried to be civil for my daughter's sake.

I leave my place at the bar and walk outside, dialing Carla's number.

"What?" she says as a greeting.

"What are you doing here, Carla?"

"I'm obviously here to see my daughter."

"Don't throw that shit at me. We both know that's not the case. What are you trying to do?"

"I don't know why you're being so cruel." Fake tears fill her voice, and I roll my eyes toward the heavens. "I just want to see Rachel. I've missed out on so much."

"By choice," I remind her.

"Are you telling me I'm not welcome in Rachel's life? That you both just want me to *leave?*"

Yes. Yes, that's what I'm fucking saying.

But it's not entirely up to me. Rachel is old enough to make her own choices regarding who she wants to have relationships with, so long as it doesn't harm her—especially when it comes to her biological mother.

"I don't like that you decided to show up out of the blue, without any warning, and interrupted our lives. I don't think you have innocent motives at all. I *don't* want you here, and if push comes to shove, I can get a restraining order. *But*…I'll let Rachel decide if she wants to spend time with you."

"She will." Carla sounds confident when she sniffs into the phone. "We have a lot of catching up to do. Maybe I should come to your place on the water for dinner tonight."

I narrow my eyes. "You are *not* welcome in my home. I don't want you anywhere near it. I'm not going to invite you over for a chummy meal. We're not friends, Carla."

"I gave you a *baby.*"

"And then you left her."

Carla hangs up on me, and I let out a sigh.

I know her too well. She doesn't want Rachel. She wants to mess with me, and she's jealous of Maeve.

She's jealous of *everything*.

Which I don't understand because she's been with Danny Kirkland for *years*. He's not a particularly successful fighter in the industry, but he makes a shit ton of money and keeps Carla in the lifestyle she always wanted.

It doesn't matter.

I want her gone.

"ARE you going to sleep at all?" Maeve reaches out and drags her hand up and down my arm in the darkness. I have the balcony door open so I can hear the waves crashing below, and the mattress is heated to keep us warm.

I usually sleep like a damn baby in this room.

But my brain won't shut down.

"I'm fine," I reply softly. "Go back to sleep."

"You're not fine." Maeve sits up and scoots closer. Having her with me is soothing in and of itself. If I were alone, I'd be in the basement, punching the bag I hung down there last week.

I can't *wait* for the gym to be finished.

"She just got home," I inform her and push my hand through my hair. "Rachel walked through the door not even thirty minutes ago. It's almost one in the goddamn morning. What in the hell could they have been doing this late?"

"Maybe they were just talking," Maeve suggests. "Catching up, like Carla said earlier."

"I don't trust her," I say, watching the white waves in the dark. "Like I said before, I don't talk shit about Carla in front of Rachel because it's up to my daughter to decide what she thinks of her mom. But Carla is a bad person, Maeve. She's manipulative and selfish. And I'm worried that all she's going to do here is hurt Rachel. All because she's pissed that *I'm* doing well."

"Why is she pissed about that?" Maeve asks. "I don't get it. Why does she *care*?"

"Who knows? Because she's unhappy, and she wants everyone else to be unhappy, too. Or she just wants *me* to be unhappy because I got what I wanted. I got Rachel."

"I sincerely hope that you're wrong, for Rachel's sake," she replies. "I hope that Carla has matured with age and realizes that she has an awesome daughter that she needs to get to know. And that she's here for that reason only—because she's missed out on a great kid."

I turn to her and cup her cheek in the darkness.

"You're such a good woman. You try to see the best in people and give them the benefit of the doubt, even when they don't deserve it."

"I don't know her," she says simply. "I don't know if she deserves Rachel. From what you've told me, I'd say not. But, like I said, I hope she's grown up and is here with good intentions. Because I promise you, if she hurts that sweet girl in *any* way, I'll tear her fucking hair out."

I grin and lean into her, kissing her neck. I need to be with her.

"Protective, aren't you?"

"Of the people I love? Hell, yes. I know you're strong, but so am I. And I don't stand for anyone hurting those I care about."

"I'm so happy that you love her."

She takes my cheeks in her hands, and with the moonlight dancing on her face, she smiles softly. "I love both of you, Hunter. Haven't you figured that out?"

I slide her down onto the bed and quietly make love to her with soft touches and breathless sighs. I moan at the tenderness of her touch and feel my heartbeat quicken when I'm inside her, pushing us both toward the ecstasy of climax.

And when it's calm again, when Maeve sleeps soundly, and I lie awake listening to the water, I'm at peace in the knowledge that we can face whatever chaos Carla brings our way.

Together.

"I DIDN'T KNOW what to expect," Rachel says to Maeve and me the next morning over bagels and cream cheese. "I don't honestly know Carla all that well. I don't see her often, you know? I mean, she's always been nice to me, she just doesn't come around much. Oh, and there was the embarrassing thing that happened at school. That was *awful.*"

Rachel spreads cream cheese on her garlic bagel, and Maeve and I share a look.

"But we stayed up super late, just talking and catching up. She's so nice, you know? She really wanted to know all about everything that's going on, and she's happy for me, that I like it here and everything."

"That's great," Maeve says with a big smile. "I'm glad you had a good time. We were a little worried, though. You didn't text your dad."

"Oh, it's okay. I was just with Mom."

Now she's calling her *mom?*

"Dad," Rachel continues, happy as can be. "Can I have a car?"

"A *what?*" I stare at her as if she's lost her mind. "You can't even drive, Rach."

"But I'm almost sixteen," she reminds me. "It's legal for me to get a permit. It didn't really matter when we lived in Seattle because we had the public transpo, but there isn't any here on the island. I'd like to be able to get around without always asking for a ride."

"I'm not even going to entertain the idea of getting you your own car until you've been through driver's ed. We'll look into it this fall. I don't have a problem with you driving, but let's not get carried away. First thing's first."

"I don't *have* to take driver's ed to test for the license. Mom said so."

I narrow my eyes and want to punch the wall.

Carla isn't the fucking driver's ed police.

"My rule says you *do* have to take driver's ed," I reply. "You've never been behind the wheel, Rach. You're nowhere near ready to take a driving test. But we'll get the ball rolling."

"Okay." She sighs in disappointment and takes a bite of her bagel. "I think I'll go walk on the beach for a while."

"Be careful," Maeve calls out to Rachel as the girl leaves the room, then she turns to me. "So, this is fun."

"I'm canceling the Vegas gig. There's no way that I can leave here in two days with Carla in town. I don't fucking trust her."

"I know you don't trust her, but you *do* trust me. And I'm telling you that we'll be okay. It's twenty-four hours. I can handle things for that long."

I pace the kitchen in frustration. "It's not *you* I'm worried about."

"Does Carla have a history of kidnapping or child endangerment?"

"No."

"Has she ever put Rachel in a dangerous situation?"

"No."

"I know she's not a great person, but I don't think she means Rachel harm. You should go. Do the job and then come back. It'll be fine."

I was looking forward to going to the fight. To seeing everyone again, hearing the crowd, and submerging myself in the life once more, even if only for a few hours.

"I'll go," I say at last. "But if there are *any* issues, I want you to call me right away. I can be home in a few hours."

"Don't worry," she says and pats me on the shoulder. "We've got this. Rachel won't do anything to hurt *me*. I'm confident in that."

"I hope you're right."

"Dad, you're going to build a gym *this* big?" Rachel asks the following day. We're standing out in the field that's just to the right of the house. It's close enough to walk to in any weather, without being right on top of the house and garage.

"That's right," I reply. "I need it to be big because I plan to put a ring inside."

"Who are you going to fight?" Maeve asks with a laugh. "It's not like we have a huge MMA population on the island."

"I'll have visitors, and I have friends from Seattle

who'll come visit. It won't go unused. Besides, I have the space and the money, so why not?"

"Can't argue with that," Maeve says as she walks around the foundation that's already been poured. "What else will it have?"

"The usual weights and cardio machines. And I think I'll put an office upstairs. Mostly, it'll be a place to display trophies and memorabilia."

"You should display those things in the house," Maeve says.

"I think it would be cool to have it all in the gym," Rachel says, thinking it over. "Like, this is where it all started and came from, and if it's part of the décor, that would be awesome."

"You know what?" Maeve says, nodding. "You're right. I like that, too. Where do you have that stuff now?"

"In boxes," I reply.

"In boxes," Maeve echoes and then laughs. "Of course, you do. Well, I'm glad you plan to put them on display. You should. You earned them."

I grin and shove my hands into my pockets. "Damn right, I did."

"I'm hungry," Rachel announces.

"You're always hungry," Maeve says and loops her arm around my daughter's shoulders. "You must be growing. That's what my mom used to say when we were growing up. What can I fix you? Tuna sandwich? Flatbread pizza?"

"The pizza sounds good," Rachel says with a grin. "Do we have pepperoni?"

"What else do you put on pizza?" Maeve asks. "Oh, Hunter, I was going to ask you a question."

"Shoot."

"Do you mind if I have my sisters and a couple of the cousins from Seattle over tomorrow night while you're gone for a little girls' night? We've been trying to arrange it since you and I went to LA, but something always comes up. Tomorrow night works for the others. There will be some alcohol, but we're never crazy with it, and we'll be responsible with Rachel here."

"They're almost all *mothers*," Rachel reminds us both. "Of course, they're not going to get wild and crazy. They're old."

Maeve and I blink at each other and then bust up laughing.

"Thanks," Maeve says and pulls Rach down in a chokehold, rubbing her knuckles in Rachel's hair. "You little jerk."

"I meant it in a nice way!" Rachel giggles and pulls out of Maeve's hold. "You look really good for your age and everything."

"I'm only thirty-four, you toddler," Maeve retaliates and starts to chase Rachel through the field.

"Of course, I don't care if you have a little party," I say when the two quit chasing each other and stop to catch their breath. "This is your home, too."

Suddenly, I hear the light honk of a horn.

We all turn to see a brand-new blue MINI Cooper convertible pull into the driveway.

"Who's that?" Rachel asks.

"No idea," I reply. "Let's go see."

As we approach, the driver puts the top down and waves over the top of the windshield.

"It's Mom," Rachel says and picks up the pace. "This is a sweet car, Mom."

"Well, I'm so happy to hear that you think so because I bought it for you, sweet girl."

No.

Oh, hell fucking no.

"What? Are you kidding?" Rachel runs over and hugs Carla as her mother steps out of the car.

"I'm not kidding at all. You mentioned that you wanted a car, and I saw this one for sale. It's adorable and fun, just like my daughter."

"Holy crap! Dad, look! It's my very own car!"

I don't smile. I don't even look at Rachel. I just glare at the woman who gave birth to her and take a long, deep breath.

"It's cute," Maeve says, breaking the silence.

"It's a convertible," Rachel gushes. "I've literally *always* wanted a convertible. This is the best, Mom. Thank you so, so much."

"You deserve it," Carla says. "You work hard, and you're a good girl. Come on, let's go for a ride. You drive."

"No, absolutely not." I step forward, having heard enough. "Rachel doesn't even have a learner's permit, and I told her *yesterday* that she couldn't have a car until she went through driver's ed."

"That's silly," Carla says, waving me off. "She doesn't need driver's ed. She just needs someone to spend some time teaching her. I'm here, I can do it."

"I said, no," I repeat and earn a glare from my daughter. I don't give a rat's ass. "Rachel, go inside."

"But, Dad—"

"Go. Inside."

"Let's go make that lunch," Maeve says and goes in with my daughter.

"Why do you have to be such a killjoy?" Carla demands and glares at me.

"Why would you buy my kid a *car* without consulting me?"

"She's my kid, too," she replies.

"Only when it suits you. And according to the law, she's not yours. You gave up your parental rights the day after she was born. You don't get to make these kinds of decisions for her, Carla. I don't know why you're here, or what you're trying to prove, but all you're doing is creating chaos."

"I'm just trying to get to know her," Carla counters. "And spoil her a bit. I'm entitled."

"You're not entitled to *anything*. This car is inappropriate, and you know it. You just don't give a shit."

She smirks. "So, put it in the garage for safekeeping

until you decide she can have it. What's the harm? I won't take her driving if it makes you that crazy."

"Go away, Carla." I back up toward the house. "Just…go away."

CHAPTER 14

*H*e's been gone for only five hours, and so far, everything is just fine. I know Hunter was on the fence about leaving with all of the new Carla drama going on, but after I assured him once again that we'd be fine, he finally agreed to go.

I had breakfast with Rachel this morning. She wasn't thrilled that her dad wouldn't change his stance on the car situation.

There's nothing at all that I can do about that.

But I was happy to lend an ear and try to be the voice of reason. Unfortunately, I think kids are deaf to the voice of reason at her age.

I just finished showing two houses to a nice couple from Nebraska. If I had to guess, I'd say they'll go for the first one. I need to swing by my house to see how things are progressing with my roof before going back to Hunter's to check on Rachel.

I shouldn't have stopped by my place. All it does is depress me. The contractors have replaced the tarps my brothers, Cam, and Hunter pieced together with a big black one to keep all moisture out, but there's been no real progress on the actual structural repairs.

It doesn't even feel like home anymore.

I only spend a few minutes there and then head back to Hunter's to see what Rachel's up to. We both have today off from the pub, which is unusual. In fact, it's going to be just the guys at O'Callaghan's tonight because the girls are all coming to Hunter's for our party.

It was nice of Keegan to insist that he could handle things with the help of our brothers and Da. Ma said she would be perfectly fine in the kitchen.

That's the difficult thing about a family-run business. It's hard to include everyone in things because someone has to work at the pub.

So far, we've been able to figure it out.

I pull into the driveway and scowl at the MINI Cooper parked in front of the garage. Hunter made it clear to both Rachel and me last night that he doesn't want Carla here while he's gone.

And yet, here she is.

Great.

I walk inside and toss my bag onto the counter, then follow the laughter coming from upstairs. I find Rachel and her mom in Rachel's room, hanging a new set of curtains.

There's a new comforter on the bed, and a different rug on the floor.

All very different from what Rachel and I picked out together just a couple of weeks ago.

I lean on the doorjamb, cross my arms over my chest, and clear my throat.

They both turn my way.

Carla's gaze hardens, and her chin stiffens. She *knows* she shouldn't be here. She knows she's just stirring the pot.

And she seems damn pleased with herself.

"Isn't this awesome?" Rachel asks with a smile. "Mom thought I needed bolder colors in here, so she bought me all new stuff. Isn't that nice?"

I force a smile in return. "It's great. I like the navy blue. Carla, can I speak to you for a moment, please?"

I walk out of the room and hear Carla say, "*I wonder what the wicked witch wants,*" making Rachel giggle.

What a bitch.

"Yes?"

"Hunter doesn't want you here." I don't mince words or try to be nice. There's no reason to. "I'm sure you already know that."

"I'm her *mother.*"

"You don't live here," I remind her. "So, technically, you're trespassing. I don't want to make things horrible for Rachel and call the police, but I will. I have no problem doing that at all, actually. Because he does. Not. Want you here."

"He's just an ass," she hisses. "Such a controlling ass."

"Even if that's true, which it isn't, this is his property. Not yours."

"You just love this, don't you, you little gold digger?" She bares her teeth and leans in. "The sex is great, isn't it? Best there fucking is. But he'll cast you aside just like he did me. And I want to be front-row-center, watching with my own eyes when it happens. He's not in love with you, no matter how many charming, mushy speeches he gives."

"Are you done?"

"You're *nothing*." She points her finger at me. "Nothing but white trash."

"You need to go." I'm proud of how calm I sound when everything in me wants to slap this bitch across the face.

She whirls back to Rachel's room.

"Well, darling, I think I need to go ahead and go. I have lots of errands to run. Of course, you're welcome to come with me if you'd like. We can hang out together, just you and me. Make it a slumber party."

Rachel's eyes light up, and she turns to me.

"You don't need to ask *her*," Carla says. "She's not your dad."

Rachel frowns with uncertainty. "Still, I'm here with her. What do you think, Maeve?"

"Let me call your dad real quick, okay?"

"Okay."

I step out once more and call Hunter's cell phone.

"What happened?"

"Nothing." I smile and shake my head. "This is literally the only time I'll interrupt you. I'm about to make a decision, and I want to make sure it isn't the wrong one."

"What's up?"

"Rachel wants to stay the night with Carla. I don't mind if she does, but I also don't mind if you say no."

He sighs on the other end of the line. "Let her go. Jesus, I hope this fiasco ends soon. She's never stuck around this long."

"I'll tell her. Now, don't worry about a thing. Go. Enjoy your time in Vegas—well, don't enjoy it *too* much."

"It's all work, babe. You and I will come together sometime and really enjoy it."

"It's a date. Okay, talk to you later."

I turn back to Rachel's room in time to see Carla opening Rachel's shirt just a bit to show off more cleavage.

"There you go. Show what your mama gave you, girl."

Rachel blushes.

I want to rush over and fix her shirt.

"Your dad is cool with it," I say instead.

"Awesome," Rachel says with a grin. "I'll be home tomorrow way before my shift starts at the pub."

"Sounds good to me."

I walk the two to the front door and keep an eye on

them, making sure that it's Carla who gets behind the wheel to drive away.

When they're out of sight, I lean against the closed door and sigh.

I don't trust Carla.

But I trust *Rachel*. And she has my number.

In fact, just to be sure, I shoot Rachel a text.

Me: *Hey, just to remind you, I'm here if you need ANYTHING. Just a phone call away.*

I watch as the three little balls bounce on my screen as she replies. But when the reply comes, it's just a heart.

At least she saw it and knows I'm here.

"SHE BOUGHT THE KID A CAR?" Jules asks with a stunned and disgusted look in her blue eyes as she sips her lemon drop martini. "Just out of the blue, without talking to Hunter first?"

"That's right." I shake my head and set a charcuterie platter on the kitchen island.

I love that there's so much chatter, so much *life* happening in this house. When I daydreamed about buying it, I always pictured it as the perfect place to host parties.

Of course, it's not *my* house, but it's awesome, nonetheless.

Maggie and Lexi are mixing the lemon drops. Nat,

Jules, and Meg are sitting with me at the island, while Anastasia, Amelia, and Izzy tour the house.

"I bet he was damn pissed," Jules says.

"Oh, very. He made her take it back."

"Good," Natalie chimes in. "It was inappropriate. I'd be mad, too. Do you really think she's just here because she's jealous of you?"

"I do," Maggie says as she reaches for some salami and a cracker. "You should have seen the look in her eyes when she saw Maeve at the pub. If looks could kill, Maeve would be cremated and in the ground."

"It's so weird," Jules says and pops an olive into her mouth. "They were never super serious, according to what Nate told me. And then she left the baby with Hunter. Why get jealous now?"

"Because this is his first public relationship," Meg Montgomery says as she refills her martini glass. "And it has to hit right in the pride that he introduced Maeve to the world at the ESPYs, and said such nice things in his speech. He's happy. He's doing great. He has a sexy girlfriend, a good relationship, and an awesome daughter. Things that she didn't even know she wanted until Hunter got them first."

"Does *she* want a sexy girlfriend?" I ask with a grin. "Not that there's anything wrong with that."

"You know what I mean," Meg says with a laugh.

"Oh, so you're saying she's vindictive," Nat says with a nod, thinking it over. "I see that. It's pretty crappy and makes her a bad human being, but I see it."

"Let's talk about Hunter," Amelia, Anastasia's sister, says as they all join us for food and cocktails. "Specifically, the sex."

"Oh, good idea." Jules sips her drink and grins. "It's crazy good, isn't it? I mean, not that I know from experience. Nate would kill me, and I don't have a death wish. Hunter just moves like he'd be stellar in bed."

I bite my lip and feel my cheeks flush. The women all bust up laughing.

"Orgasms," Natalie says, holding up her glass in a toast. "The best thing there is."

"I think I'll text Nate and let him know that I'm gonna need some orgasms later," Jules says.

"Do you think Nate doesn't know?" Natalie quips.

"Where is Nate?" I ask. "I thought you guys were all staying on the island tonight."

"We are," Amelia says. "All the guys came. They're hanging out at the pub. Then we'll all meet up for kid-free sexy time later."

"Nice." I grin at her and glance over at Izzy, who looks amazing, but a little tired. "And how's our new mama? You look great, Iz."

"Thanks. I'm exhausted. Baby is up crying *all the time.* I feel like a horrible mother because I can't get her to settle down. I've tried everything. She'll only sleep for Keegan."

"That sucks," Jules says and pats Izzy's back. "Colic is the worst. She'll grow out of it. Have you named her?"

"No. Keegan and I are usually on the same page when it comes to just about everything, but we can't agree on this. I told him we have until the end of the month to figure it out. Her name can't be *Baby* forever."

"I heard you delivered really fast," Meg says. "I'm fascinated. Tell me everything."

"My doctor suspects I was laboring all week, and that last day, my body was like, *yep. We're doing this.* But because it just felt similar to how I felt all week, I didn't think it was different. Boy, was I wrong. I had her less than thirty minutes after my water broke."

"I'd take that," Anastasia says. "I was in labor *forever.*"

"We're old," I announce. "We're talking about child-birth on our girls' night."

"Let's go back to orgasms," Natalie suggests.

I turn when the front door suddenly opens. "Rachel?"

She comes staggering inside. She's pale, her lips are bright pink, and not from gloss or lipstick.

"Rachel, what's wrong? Did your mom drop you off?"

"Walked." She rubs her head. "I don't feel so good."

Meg steps in and examines Rachel's eyes. "Dilated. Her pulse is a bit fast. I don't have my blood pressure cuff with me. Sweetie, did you ingest something? Have you been drinking?"

Rachel's eyes fill with tears. "Didn't mean to. Mom made daiquiris for her and Danny. Then she made me one without alcohol. They started acting really weird. Like, gross. And I wanted to come home, so I walked, but then I started *feeling* weird."

"What did she put in the drinks?" Meg asks, and we lead Rachel to a couch. "Do you know?"

"She said something about an edible. Whatever that means."

I sigh and close my eyes. *Oh, you sweet, innocent girl.*

"Shit," Jules mutters. "Do we need an ambulance?"

"I don't think so," Meg says. "She needs to sleep off the high."

"Is this what it feels like to be high? Because it sucks. Why do people do this?" Rachel's eyes fill with tears. "My dad's gonna *kill* me. I didn't do it on purpose."

"He's not going to be mad at you," I assure her. "It's not your fault. Why didn't you call me? You didn't have to walk."

"Forgot my phone." She blinks slowly. "This is the weirdest thing. I think I'm sleepy."

"She'll be hungry in a bit," Natalie murmurs.

"Let's put you to bed," Maggie suggests, and we take her upstairs. Meg comes along to continue to monitor her, and when we have her all tucked in, and Rachel is snoring peacefully, we walk out, leaving the door open so I can hear her.

"You have to call Hunter," Maggie says immediately when we return downstairs.

"He's in the middle of a fight," I remind her. "He's on

live television. I can't just call him. Or even text him. She's safe now and not in the hospital or anything. I'll tell him when he gets back tomorrow."

"He's going to be seriously pissed," Lexi adds.

"I think this is exactly the kind of thing that had to happen to get Carla to go," I reply. "There's no way he'll let Rachel have anything to do with her now. It's not safe."

"What a horrible mother," Izzy says, shaking her head. "And trust me, I know what a bad mother is. Intimately. My mom sucks, big-time. But she'd never do something like that."

"I don't envy you tomorrow," Jules says. "He's not going to be happy."

"It's not like he's going to punch the walls or something," I reply. "But yeah, he'll be angry. And he should be."

"Keep an eye on her tonight," Meg says. "She should just sleep it off and wake up fine tomorrow. If I'm interpreting what she said correctly, it sounds like Carla the moron made the drinks with the cannabis for her and whoever Danny is first, and then made the virgin one for Rachel with residual stuff still in the blender."

"She's not a terribly smart baby mama, is she?" Lexi asks.

"The good thing about that is, there shouldn't have been much in Rachel's drink. Just enough to knock her out for a while."

Meg runs down the list of what to do if things go bad, and then we wrap up the party early.

It's hard to be silly and have fun when my boyfriend's fifteen-year-old minor just came home high after spending time with her mom.

I lock up, clean the kitchen, and then go up to check on Rachel.

She's turned on her side and is still sleeping well. She looks so young. So sweet.

I'm afraid to leave her.

What if there was too much in that drink and she starts to have serious issues from it?

I *can't* leave her.

So, I lie down next to her and keep an eye on her. Listen to her breathe. I smooth my fingers through her hair when she whimpers.

"It's okay, honey. I'm not going anywhere."

"I want my daddy."

"I know. He'll be home in the morning. But we're okay, you and me. I've got you."

"Glad." She licks her lips but doesn't open her eyes. "Glad you're here. Don't leave us, okay?"

"I'm not going to leave you."

"Messed up."

I cup her cheek, my heart breaking for her. "It wasn't your fault, Rach. Honest. I know you've been in trouble in the past for things that *were* your fault, but this isn't one of them. You're not in trouble. I just hate that you were alone and that you walked home. I would have come to get you. I love you so much."

Her lips tip up. "Love you. It sounds real when you say it. Not like her."

I feel a tear fall from the corner of my eye. "It's real."

She's quiet for a long moment, and I think maybe she's gone back to sleep, but then she says, "Can I have Grandda's number?"

I grin. "Sure, but he's not very good with his phone."

"I'll teach him. He's my favorite."

"I think you're *his* favorite, too. Don't worry, we won't tell the others."

I DIDN'T SLEEP MUCH, but I didn't expect to. I just lay next to Rachel, listening to her breathe. She slept all night. Didn't even make a peep.

She was fine.

But I was paranoid.

At one point, I opened her window so I could hear the ocean and then just lay there and daydreamed a bit. It was peaceful.

But now, it's time to get up and get started on the day. Intending to let Rachel sleep in, I slip from the bed and reach for my phone, but frown when it's not within reach.

I must have forgotten it downstairs last night.

I walk down, flip on the coffee maker, and reach for my cell.

I have two texts from Hunter, and one missed call.

Hunter: *Hey! Are you still awake?*

That one was just past midnight, probably when he got back to his room after the fight.

The next one was this morning.

Hunter: *Good morning, beautiful. I'm headed back to the island earlier than planned. I miss my girls, and there's nothing for me here in Vegas. I should be there no later than nine. See you soon!*

I glance at the clock. It's already past eight.

This is good news. I'm ready to sit down with Hunter and tell him what happened with his daughter yesterday.

"Maeve?"

I turn at the sound of Rachel's voice and smile softly at the teenager.

"Well, good morning sunshine."

She scratches her head and yawns. "I dreamed you were in my bed all night."

"I *was* in your bed all night." I cross to her and wrap my arms around her for a hug. "How do you feel?"

"Pretty much normal," she says. "Hungry. Can we invite your parents over for breakfast?"

I raise a brow. "Really?"

Rachel nods. "Yeah. I think it would be nice."

"Sure. I'll give them a call. Maybe you should go hop in the shower. It might help you feel even better."

"Good idea." She turns to head for the stairs, then turns back to me. "Hey, Maeve?"

"Yes, sweetie?"

"Thank you."

I nod as I reach for my phone so I can call my parents. "You're welcome."

CHAPTER 15

~HUNTER~

The ferry seemed to take *forever* to cross the Sound to the island. I was too wound up from the fight to sleep worth a damn last night, and I missed being here with Maeve and Rachel, so I decided to leave Vegas at roughly five this morning.

And now I'm back on the island, driving toward my house.

I love this place. It feels like I've always lived here. Like this is where I was supposed to be all along. Most of all, I'm relieved that Rachel is happy here and that she's thriving in this little town.

I pull into the driveway and park next to an older Ford SUV, then hurry inside. I didn't hear back from Maeve last night, but I figured she was either still having fun with her friends or had fallen asleep.

She did finally text me about an hour ago and said that she was excited to see me.

The house smells of bacon and eggs and, if I'm not mistaken, sausage gravy.

"Looks like I'm just in time," I announce as I walk into the kitchen. Fiona is manning the stove, and I can see through the window that Rachel is sitting outside with Tom.

"Good morning," Maeve says as she hurries over and wraps her arms around my neck and holds on tight. "You're a sight for sore eyes."

"I was only gone for twenty-four hours," I remind her with a laugh.

"Yeah, well, a lot has happened." She clears her throat and backs away. "We need to talk, Hunter."

"First of all, are you and Rach okay?"

"Yes, we're safe and fine," Maeve assures me.

"You know, I think I have everything done in here for now," Fiona says with a wink. "I'll just join Tom and our sweet Rachel outside. It's a beautiful morning."

She closes the door behind her, and I narrow my eyes on Maeve.

"What's going on?"

"I'm just going to tell you everything from the beginning," Maeve says as she takes a deep breath. "I came home early yesterday afternoon to find Carla here. *In* the house, Hunter. She was in Rachel's room, and they were setting up all-new décor. Rachel said her mom bought her all new stuff."

I cross my arms over my chest and listen as my blood begins to fucking boil.

"I asked her to leave," Maeve continues, "after some nasty words from her—all out of range of Rachel, of course. Anyway, that's when I called and asked if Rach could stay with Carla."

"Okay."

"After they left, I sent Rach a text and reminded her that I was only a phone call away in case she needed anything. Then I went about my day. The girls came over, and we had a couple of drinks and some food. It was nice."

"I'm glad." I feel my stomach tighten because I have a feeling the other shoe is about to drop.

"At about nine, Rachel suddenly came through the door—"

Before she can continue, my daughter hurries in from outside with tears in her eyes. She leaves the door wide-open so Fiona and Tom can hear. "I swear to you, it wasn't my fault. I didn't *know*."

Maeve sighs and closes her eyes, then keeps talking.

"I haven't told him all of it yet," Maeve says.

"I seriously didn't know," Rachel continues.

"Hold on." I hold up a finger, and Rachel stops talking. "Maeve, finish it."

"She came home," Maeve continues. "She *walked* home, Hunter. She was acting odd and said she didn't feel good. Said that Carla and Danny were making her uncomfortable, and she just wanted to come home."

"Whoa." I shake my head. "*Danny* was there?"

"Yes," Rachel whispers.

"That's not the worst of it," Maeve says. "Apparently, they made a blended drink for themselves and added edible marijuana to it. Then, without cleaning the blender, they made a *virgin* drink for Rachel."

"Except it wasn't virgin," I finish for her.

"No," Maeve agrees. "It wasn't."

"They were high and acting so stupid. I didn't want to be there anymore," Rachel says, picking up the story. "I was mad, actually. So, I just left. But when I was about halfway home, I started to feel really weird. I couldn't call Maeve because I forgot my phone at Carla's."

She's back to calling her Carla. That's good.

"She was pretty stoned when she got here," Maeve says. "Meg Montgomery is a nurse and evaluated her. She just had to sleep it off. So, she did."

"Did Carla ever call here last night, wondering where Rachel was?"

Both girls just blink at me, and that's all the answer I need.

I don't know that I've ever felt so much fucking rage in all of my damn life.

I have to leave the room. I want to yell and throw a fucking fit, and that won't solve anything. It will likely only upset everyone more.

I stomp out the open back door and make it all the way to the cliffs before I realize that Tom has followed. He moves a bit slower, but he joins me on the cliffs.

"I'd wager that you're good and angry right now."

"You'd win that bet."

He nods. "Maeve said she didn't want to call you when it all happened because you were in the middle of doing your job. The fight was still going, and it was live television."

I blow out a breath and shove my hands through my hair with frustration.

"She still should have called."

"I don't disagree. It's a scary thing that I'd say no one expected to happen. It scared your daughter, and that's the truth of it."

"Are we sure this isn't another stunt of hers?" I ask and turn to Tom. "Rachel was famous for pulling shit like this when we lived in Seattle."

"T'wasn't, no." Tom shakes his head. "She asked Fiona and me to come to breakfast this morning and told us about it. She said Maeve slept with her all night to make sure she was okay."

"I'm grateful that she did that. And I'm damn disgusted that she had to."

"You have two good girls in there, son. I know you're angry, and you've got good reason to be. I'd be livid meself. But it's not their fault. You need to take this up with the person responsible."

"You're right."

I pull my phone out of my pocket as Tom walks back toward the house and dial Carla's number.

"Hello?"

"What the fuck were you thinking?"

"Huh?" I hear her fumbling around. "What time is it?"

"Rachel's safe, in case you were wondering."

"Of course, she is. She's with me."

"No. She's fucking *not*. She's home, where she belongs. Because you and that asshole, Danny, were too high last night to know what the fuck was going on. There was enough of the drugs still in the blender that it made my daughter high, as well."

"What are you even talking about?" she demands. "You're making all of this up."

"No. I'm not. And I have witnesses. You're done, do you hear me? Fucking *done*. You won't have any contact with Rachel. You won't come to see her. You signed over your rights to her years ago, and you have no place in her life. If you try to keep up this stupid charade, I'll make your life a living hell."

"Are you *threatening* me?"

"No. I'm telling you how it is. Stay away from my kid, Carla. Or you'll regret it."

I hang up and turn to find Maeve walking toward me.

"I'm sorry," she says before I can say anything. "I should have called, but I didn't know what to do. I didn't know what was right. And all I wanted was to keep my eyes on her in case something went really wrong."

I reach for her, tug her into my arms, and hold her tightly against me.

"I just love her so much," she keeps going and sniffles against my chest. "And I was so worried. I want to punch that bitch in her smug little face. She called me a *gold digger* for fuck's sake, Hunter."

"What?" That makes me laugh. "Of all of the things you are, babe, a gold digger isn't one of them."

"I *know*. And who is Danny?"

I have a bitter taste in my mouth at just the mention of the asshole's name.

"Carla's been with Danny for years. I don't think they're married. Not sure." I shrug. "Don't really care, honestly. He's a fighter, and not a particularly good one. I've fought him several times. Always kick his ass."

"Good."

I smile. "He's a dick. He talks a lot of smack—more than normal for someone who rarely wins. He's not a champion. He doesn't have what it takes to be a champion. Clearly, the asshole does drugs for fuck's sake."

"What are you going to do?" she asks.

"I already called Carla and told her she can have no more contact with Rachel."

"I figured you'd do that."

"I need to have a talk with my kid, too. Is there any food left?"

"Ma's inside warming up everything now." Maeve takes a deep breath of sea air. "It was awful last night. How is this possible?"

"How is what possible?" I reach over and tuck her red hair behind her ear.

"I've only known you for…what? Less than two months?"

"About that."

"And I'm completely in love with you. With both of you. I'm possessive and protective. So protective. It's like I've been with you for years. Forever."

"It's not always about time," I remind her. "I've been in love with you since the first time I saw you at the pub. And then the next day, when you were all prim and proper, and trying to sell me any house but this one."

She laughs and glances back at the house. "Well, it's *my* dream house."

"And it's yours."

Her smile fades. "It's *your* house, Hunter."

"And you live in it. Do you really think I'm going to let you leave when the repairs on the other house are finished? Not a chance in hell."

She props her hands on her hips in that sassy way she does that makes me fucking crazy. Her lips tip up in a smile.

"What am I supposed to do with the other house?"

"Sell it, rent it out, keep it for family to use. Hell, I don't care. I just want you with us. In your dream house."

"I mean, it's a *really* nice house, so I guess I could put up with you in exchange for living in it."

I grab her wrist, haul her over my shoulder, and take off toward the house.

"What the hell?" She giggles and pats my butt. "Put me down, you caveman."

"Eventually," I reply, but carry her until we get to the house, then set her on her feet in the kitchen.

Three pairs of eyes turn to us.

"Is there any bacon left?" I ask.

"I HAVE A DELIVERY FOR RACHEL MEYERS," the kid says when I answer the door.

"I'm her dad."

He passes me a padded envelope and then leaves. I rip it open, and Rachel's phone falls out, along with a note from Carla.

"Rach!" I call up the stairs and open the note.

Rachel,

I don't know what happened last night. I'm very disappointed in you for leaving without telling me. You got me into big trouble with your dad! He says I have to stay away, but don't worry, you and I will come up with a little plan.

I've saved a new number in your phone under the name Trina. *So you can still talk to me. Just tell Hunter it's a friend from school. We will outsmart him!*

Keep me posted on all the things we talked about. And text me later!

Mom

I open her phone and delete Trina and Carla's

number, then climb the steps to see what Rachel's up to. I'll be shredding the note.

I should have figured that Carla would try to find a way to go behind my back.

"Rach?" I knock on her door and then open it, blinking in surprise.

Maeve and my daughter are hanging curtains and dancing to an old Britney Spears song.

"Hey, Dad," Rachel says with a grin. "We're just putting my stuff back up. I'm gonna throw the crap Carla bought in the trash."

"I think that about does it," Maeve says as she fusses with a pillow on the bed. "Back to normal. We have to go to the pub in just a little bit."

"Do I have time to chat with my daughter?" I ask.

"Of course. I'm going to go change my clothes." Maeve walks to me and kisses my cheek, then leaves us alone.

"Is that my phone?" Rachel asks, gesturing to the cell in my hand.

"It is. Your—Carla had it sent over for you."

"Sweet." Rachel takes the offered phone and checks it for messages, then tucks it into her pocket.

"Honey, did Carla try to get you to go along with some scheme she dreamed up?"

The smile on my daughter's face fades, and she sits on her bed. "Sort of, yeah. She kept talking about me coming to live with her. Said I could just sneak away."

"Run away."

"Yeah. But I knew it wouldn't really happen. Carla has always talked like that, even when I was little."

My head snaps up. "What?"

"She's just full of it, Dad. She always has been. Oh, I found out yesterday that she didn't buy that Cooper. She rented it. She just wanted to piss you off."

"Jesus." I drag my hand down my face in frustration. "It worked."

"And she *hates* Maeve. Like, whenever I talked about Maeve and her family, Carla would tell me to shut my mouth. She's so jealous. And I swear I didn't know that Danny was going to show up. He's such a creep. I don't like the way he looks at me."

I narrow my eyes. "And how is that?"

"In a creepy, old-dude way. And he's not very nice."

"No. He isn't."

"Anyway, I'm sorry about last night, Dad. I know I've been in trouble for things like this before, although I've never done any kind of drugs. But I swear to you, this time, it was *not* my fault."

"I know." I sigh and reach over to ruffle her hair. "I know it wasn't. Rach, I told Carla she can't see you again. It's just not safe. For as long as you're a minor and live with me, I won't allow it."

"Good." She sighs in relief. "Because last night sucked, and I have no interest in seeing her. I thought I had to because she's my mom."

"Nope, you don't have to. She has no legal right to you."

"Okay. I think it's best if she just goes away and doesn't come back."

"I agree. I'm glad we're on the same page here. Now, I need to talk to you about something else."

"Oh, geez, what did I do now?"

I laugh and tug her in for a quick hug. "Nothing, you little stink bug. I want to talk about Maeve. I know it might seem like it's moving fast, but I want her here with us. Permanently."

"Like, are you going to marry her?"

"God, I hope so."

Rachel grins. "I love her, Dad. Like, I really love her. And her family is just the best. Grams and Gramps like them, too. I want her family to be part of ours."

"I take it that means you're okay with it, then?"

Rachel rolls her eyes and makes me chuckle. "Yeah. I'm great with it."

CHAPTER 16

~MAEVE~

Someone is licking my neck.

I grin and remember all of the mornings that my brother's dog, Murphy, woke me up by licking my toes.

But he's never licked my neck.

I crack open an eye and find Hunter nuzzling me, his hand gliding over my skin from hip to breast and back again. Good God, the things this man can do with his hands should be illegal in at least four states.

Maybe five.

"Good morning." His voice is gruff with sleep. The light stubble on his cheek scratches over my skin.

It's not unpleasant in the least.

"Morning. I thought you were Murphy."

He lifts his head and scowls down at me. "Who the fuck is Murphy?"

"My brother's dog."

His eyes narrow. "You thought I was a *dog*?"

I giggle and play with the hair at the nape of his neck. "I was sleeping really hard. I wasn't in my right mind."

"I'm going to keep you out of your right mind for a while," he promises and goes back to trailing kisses down my chest to one nipple. My back bows in invitation, and I moan when his hand finds its way between my legs. "Do you like that, babe?"

"You know I do." My voice is breathy now, and my skin heats as he covers me and settles himself between my legs.

"You're too beautiful in the morning," he murmurs. "I couldn't resist you."

"You've always been charming." I grin and then sigh when he glides the head of his cock over my slick lips. "Waking up like this does not suck."

"I was hoping you'd feel that way." His lips are gentle on mine as he sinks inside of me. He braces his elbows on the bed, his fingers tangling in my hair as he starts to move. "I can't get enough of you, Maeve. I want you constantly. I crave you."

The words are an aphrodisiac all on their own. My body is on fire.

"All of this, every delectable inch of you, is *mine,* Maeve O'Callaghan." His eyes pin mine, his gaze intense. "Do you understand?"

"Perfectly."

I grip his ass and urge him to move faster, but he

maintains his lazy, slow pace. I'm pretty sure he's trying to drive me absolutely insane.

"Faster."

"No." He bites my chin. "I'm enjoying you."

"Enjoy me faster."

He smiles against my neck. God, I love it when he does that.

"That's totally against the whole point of lazy morning sex."

I gasp when he grinds the root of his cock against my clit, and that little piece of metal from heaven hits me in *just* the right spot, making me see stars.

"Holy shit," I mumble.

"That the spot?"

"Oh, holy shit." I fist the linens and lift my legs. When he slides out, slow as can be, and then inside once more, I see more stars and completely explode.

"Fuck, yes," he says, his body tight with the tension of his release.

"I really have to express my gratitude," I swallow hard as he rolls to the side. "For the immense discomfort you must have gone through to get that piercing. Because holy hell, it does something for me."

He laughs and scratches his fingers over the stubble on his chin. "It was a nightmare back in the day. Hurt like a bitch, and took about six months to heal."

"Good God, I would have taken it out."

"Well, what would have been the point of that? I just

would have gone through the pain for nothing. Once it healed, it was fine."

"I can't even have earrings in my *ears*." I yawn into my hand. "They get infected."

"Haven't I seen you in earrings?" he asks.

"They're clip-ons." I sit up and let the sheet fall around my waist, exposing my breasts to the cool morning air.

Hunter leans over to circle my nipple with the tip of his tongue and then draws it between his teeth but doesn't bite down hard.

"I need to get ready," I tell him.

"For what?"

"I have three showings this morning, and then I have to work at the pub this evening."

"That's a long day," he comments as I stand from the bed and begin gathering the clothes I plan to wear today. "Are you still okay with it?"

"With what? Working a full day?"

"I guess."

I glance over at him. "What's the alternative?"

"I'm just throwing it out there that you don't *have* to work two jobs."

"I didn't *have* to before, Hunter. I like the pub, and I like to sell houses. I have time for both."

"I'm just clarifying that it's what you still want."

"Yep. I enjoy it all."

I walk into the bathroom and turn on the shower so the water can warm up. I've never considered giving up either of my jobs. Keegan needs me at the pub, and it's only a few nights a week.

And real estate is my passion.

I'll do both for as long as I possibly can.

Hunter strolls into the bathroom and wraps his arms around me from behind, kissing my neck as he steps into my hot shower.

"Hey! I had that running for *me.*"

"Finders keepers." He winks and tips his head back to wet his hair. "You're welcome to join me."

"I don't have time for more fun." I cross my arms over my naked chest and tap my toe. "You know, your work question kind of pissed me off."

"Why?" He clears the steam from the shower door and frowns at me. "It was just a question. I don't want you to burn out."

"Because I've had the two jobs since before I met you. For quite a while, actually. And I juggle both just fine. I *like* it."

"Then you should keep doing it. I just wanted to point out that you don't *have* to if you're doing it for financial reasons."

"Do you think I'm poor because I work at the pub?"

"I don't think you're hurting," he says, thinking it over. "That wasn't my point."

"I made over half a million last year from real estate," I inform him. "I do just fine. I work at the pub because I enjoy my family. It's that simple."

"Wow, good for you." Hunter clears the steam again and grins at me. "That's awesome. You're good at it."

"Yes. I am. And even if I was struggling financially, I wouldn't just assume that I could quit one of my jobs and live off you. I'm not a *gold digger.*"

"Okay." He opens the door, grabs my wrist, and yanks me into the shower with him. He presses me against the cool tile and tips up my chin. "That wasn't some kind of fucked-up test, Maeve. I know who you are. You said you'd slept really well, and you look a little tired today. I only want to make sure you're not burning out. End of story."

"Sorry for getting prickly. I guess Carla's comment pissed me off more than I realized."

"Don't let it. It doesn't matter what she says or what she thinks."

"You're right." He moves under the spray to rinse his hair. "Now, hurry up. I have work to do."

"Do you have time to meet the builder with me today?" he asks, surprising me.

"Sure. What time?"

"In about an hour?"

I juggle some things around in my head. "Actually, that works. I have a showing only about a block from here. You know that blue house just down the street?"

"I know it."

"I can come back here after that. Actually, do you mind popping in there when you're ready for me?"

His eyes narrow on me. "You know I don't mind, but why?"

"There's something about this client that I don't like. I'd like to have you there, just in case he turns out to be a creep."

"I'll be there."

"As you can see, there's no direct water view in this home, but you're only a block away from beach access."

"Hmm." My client nods and continues circling the kitchen, his hands clasped behind his back, his creepy eyes moving back to me every few seconds.

I check the time. Hunter should be stopping by any minute.

"Did you want to see the garage?" I ask as he circles the island yet again.

"No, it's not the garage that I'm interested in."

"Uh, okay. You've been really quiet. I'm honestly not sure if you like the place or not."

"I'm going to be frank." He turns to me, and his gaze slithers up and down my frame, making me instantly feel physically sick. "I'd like to fuck you on this island."

"That's not included in the purchase price."

"Oh, come on. We can work something out. I've seen you look at me. You want me, you little slut."

"And...we're done," I announce, my heels clicking

smartly on the hardwood as I march to the front door. "You can go fuck yourself."

"Hey, I hired you. That means you do what I tell you to do."

"No. It doesn't." I reach for the door, but before I can get my hand on the knob, he jerks me back by the hair and slams me against the wall. I bring my knee up but miss his balls by about two inches.

"You're nothing but a tease," he hisses.

"I haven't been flirting with you, Dale. Let me go."

There's a knock on the door, and I immediately scream. Hunter slams the door open, and when he sees that Dale has me pinned against the wall, he pounces on the other man, punching him in the eye as he drags his ass outside.

Hunter tosses Dale toward the man's car.

"Get the fuck out of here," Hunter growls. "Before I fucking kill you."

Dale scurries to his car, holding his right eye. Hunter turns back to me.

"Are you hurt?"

"No."

"Did he put his hands on you?"

"Just barely. It was mostly what he said. God, what a piece of shit. Thanks for coming."

Hunter pulls me into his arms and holds on tight. "No more showing houses to single men alone."

"I won't," I agree and take a long, deep breath. "I promise."

∿

IT'S A MONDAY NIGHT, which means we're busy with baseball lovers catching the game on our big-screen TVs and eating all of the good food out of the kitchen.

We've been going pretty much nonstop for a few hours, and Rachel looks exhausted. She's been working like crazy over the past couple of weeks since Carla left, and life has settled down considerably. Rachel has her dad's work ethic. There's no doubt about it.

"Hey, why don't you take a break?" I suggest. "Go sit at the bar and chat with Grandda for a few. Your feet are killing you."

"How do you know?" Rachel asks.

"Because this isn't my first rodeo. Go take a break. We can handle this."

Rachel smiles gratefully and hops up onto a seat at the bar. My dad grins from ear to ear and pours her a root beer.

I hurry into the kitchen and am surprised to find only Maggie and Cameron.

Cameron curses under his breath and turns to leave.

"This conversation isn't over, Mary Margaret," he promises and storms out of the room.

I turn to my sister. "What's wrong?"

"Nothing. I'm fine. Everything's fine. It's all bloody fine." She tosses her hands into the air and storms out after him, leaving me completely confused.

"Where is Shawn?"

"I'm here," Shawn says and walks out of the refrigerator, carrying bags of fries. "I wanted to give them some privacy."

"What were they saying?"

Shawn turns and stares at me. "How should I know? I was giving them privacy."

"You're really bad at this," I inform him before I pull my order out from under the warmer and load my tray.

I've just stepped out from the kitchen when I see that Carla is walking over to Rachel with a big, muscular man in tow.

Jesus, what is she doing here? There's been *nothing* from her, zero contact, for weeks. Why is she back?

I set the tray down and pull out my phone to text Hunter.

Me: *Need you at the pub ASAP. Carla's here.*

I hurry over in time to hear Carla greet Rachel.

"Hey there, darling. I haven't heard from you. I was getting worried."

"I'm not supposed to talk to you," Rachel says, her voice low. She won't look her mother in the face. She's hunched over, staring down at the bar.

"Well, that's just silly. I'm your mama."

My dad steps closer. "The lass just told you she isn't to speak with you. I'd appreciate it if you'd leave my pub."

Rachel swallows hard.

"Are you going to let this old, stupid man tell me

what to do?" Carla demands of Rachel, and the teenager immediately stands up out of her chair, fury radiating off of her in waves.

"Don't you *dare* talk about my family that way," Rachel says, getting in her mom's face. "He's not an *old man.* He's a wonderful man, and I love him. And he loves *me.* For real. Not like you. I don't want anything to do with you and your trashy boyfriend. I want you to *go.* Just go."

Suddenly, Danny grips Rachel's arm above the elbow and pushes his face into hers. "Don't you *ever* talk to your mom that way again, you little ungrateful bitch."

Keegan jumps over the bar, and Cameron reaches over to grab Danny by the collar, but the man is suddenly walking backwards, though not under his own power.

Hunter's dragging him.

We all follow to see what will happen, and I pray that I don't have to call the police—or an ambulance.

"If you *ever* touch my daughter again, I'll end you," Hunter says, his voice steely and calm.

Danny holds his hands out at his sides. "Go ahead and punch me, you chickenshit."

"You're not worth it. If either of you comes back inside, we'll call the police. And I'll be getting a restraining order," Hunter informs Carla. "Don't ever come back on this island."

"I'll sue you!" Carla rails. "I'll take you for everything you've got!"

We all ignore her and walk back into the pub where Rachel's wiping away tears and talking to my father.

She didn't follow us outside.

"Did you kill him?" Rachel asks her dad. "Oh, God, I don't want you to go to jail."

"No." Hunter kisses her head. "They're leaving. I'll get some legal paperwork going as soon as I leave here."

"Come on now, lass," Dad says to Rachel. "Let's go see what kind of cake Fiona made today. That always makes everything a wee bit better."

The two of them, with their heads together, walk back to the kitchen.

"It's really sweet," Maggie says, watching them, "how cute they are together. Two peas in a pod. And she just stood right up for him when that asshole insulted Da."

"They love each other," I say simply.

"I DON'T REMEMBER the last time we had a quiet night in," I say a week later. All three of us are home, sitting in the game room upstairs.

I'm reading a book, and Hunter challenged Rachel to a game of ping-pong.

It's all so...*normal*.

"Can I go to the movies with Charity tomorrow night?" Rachel asks as she volleys the little white ball back to her dad.

"Who's Charity?"

"The girl I met at the pub. She came in yesterday with her parents for dinner. She's in my grade, and she seems cool. I need to make new friends."

Hunter glances at me. "Do you know Charity?"

"I've seen her around town quite a bit. I know she volunteers at the animal shelter in the summer. Maggie was considering a kitten, and we saw her there."

"Okay, I suppose you can go." Rachel wins the set and makes her father scowl. Before they can start another match, Hunter's phone rings. "It's my agent."

He sets the paddle down and answers.

"Hello." Hunter's eyebrows lower in a scowl. "You're kidding. Yeah, yeah, I'm looking."

He grabs the remote and turns on the TV, flipping the channel to ESPN.

There's Danny, sitting at a table, answering questions.

"Look, the jerk gave me a black eye," Danny says, pointing to his face.

"That's a lie," Hunter growls. "I didn't fucking hit him, but I sure as hell should have."

"And," Danny continues, "I'd like to settle this like gentlemen. In the ring. I want Meyers to come out of retirement for one last fight."

"Do you think he'll accept?" a reporter calls out.

"I don't know," Danny says. "He's been a bit of a pansy these last few years. We'll see if he's up for the challenge."

"Fuck him!" Hunter exclaims. "I'm in. Arrange it."

Hunter cuts off the call and tosses his phone on the couch.

"You don't have to take his bait," I point out calmly.

"He just challenged me on *national* television. What would you have me do?"

"I'm just saying, if you don't want to fight him, you don't have to."

"Oh, trust me, I want to beat that asshole's face in. I'll take great pleasure in it."

I stand and pace the room. "Listen, I know that you made fighting a living. The *sport* of fighting. This is something else entirely. This isn't a fight for sport, it's a vendetta."

"I never should have retired," Hunter mutters and rubs his hand down his face. "I wasn't ready."

"You retired for Rachel," I remind him and look at the girl who's watching us with avid curiosity.

"Partly," he agrees. "But mostly it was because the doctors told me if I got one more concussion, I might not recover from another brain injury."

I stare at him, stunned. "You never told me that."

"It's not a secret. I just didn't mention it."

"So you're saying if you get another brain injury, you could *die* from it?"

"Or be a vegetable." He pushes his hands through

his hair in agitation. "Trust me, that asshole won't hit my head."

"You don't know that. This isn't worth risking your life for."

He narrows his eyes at me.

"Are you saying that if I do this, you won't support me?"

I growl in frustration and shake my head. "No. I'm not saying that. I'll support you no matter what. I *am* saying that I want you to really think this over and not just jump in headfirst because of a knee-jerk reaction."

Hunter licks his lips. "Maeve, I love you. And I hear you. But I'm doing this. Because, yes, this is personal. I want it."

"Well, then, I guess that's that." I blow out a nervous breath. I want to talk him out of it. I want to beg him not to do this. But I see the determination written all over his face, and I know that he's made up his mind.

I don't want to lose him.

IT'S BEEN two weeks since Danny challenged Hunter to a fight. Two weeks of Hunter working out and training like a man possessed. The gym is just a shell, not yet sheetrocked and finished, but Hunter had equipment hauled in so he could begin to use it immediately.

He's out in that gym more than he's anywhere else. And that includes spending time with Rachel and me.

I walk out to the building and open the door, finding Hunter on the treadmill, sweat running down his torso in rivulets.

"Hey," I say and wave to get his attention.

"Hi." He slows down the treadmill and reaches for a white towel to wipe off his face. "What's up?"

"Everyone will be here in about thirty minutes for Rachel's party, remember?"

"Oh, shit. I lost track of time." He checks his watch. "Sorry, I'll hit the shower and get ready."

He jumps off the treadmill, and I expect him to pull me close, and kiss me silly. But he doesn't. He just smiles and walks right past me.

And it hurts my damn feelings.

But I have a party to host for a gorgeous sixteen-year-old, and she deserves to have a great day, so I make my way back to the house to finish getting ready.

Hunter makes good on his word and is just hurrying down the stairs when his parents ring the doorbell. It seems everyone arrives at once, and before long, we have a packed house, full of chaos and laughter.

It's a balm to my nervous soul.

"What's wrong?" Shawn asks when he gets me alone in the kitchen. I'm putting candles on the cake.

"What do you mean?"

"Come on, Maeve. I know you inside and out, and I can see that you're a little miserable. What's up? Does your house have more problems?"

"Always." I chuckle and shake my head. "I'm worried about Hunter. And me, if I'm being honest. He's so intent on this upcoming fight, it's all he thinks about. He's consumed with training, with the way he's eating. Rachel said he's never been this way before. It's different this time. Not that I would know because this is the first fight I've seen him get ready for."

"It's a personal one this time," Shawn says. He's always the voice of reason. "The man hurt his daughter, Maeve. Put her in danger, and then had his hands on her at the pub. If it was me, or anyone else in our family, we'd do the same. You know that."

"I've resolved myself to the fight," I reply. "I understand why he needs to do it. I just hate feeling disconnected from him."

"Talk to him." Shawn pats my shoulder. "That's all you can do. Talk it out. And give me some of that cake."

"Rachel has to blow out the candles first."

"Well, let's get a move on because I saw Da eyeing it earlier as well."

"What is it with this family and cake?"

It doesn't take long before Rachel has blown out the candles, and while we all enjoy the vanilla cake with buttercream frosting, the birthday girl tears through her presents.

"A new phone," she exclaims and smiles brilliantly at her father. "Thanks, Dad. Does this one have the tracking app on it, too?"

Hunter's face turns into a scowl. "How did you know about that?"

"Duh. I know more about phones than *you* do."

"Just leave the app on, and no one gets hurt."

Rachel rolls her eyes, but everyone laughs. It's been a fun party, and I can see by Rachel's big smile that she feels special and loved.

That's the goal.

And once everyone has left, and I've cleaned the kitchen, I go in search of Hunter to sit with him and have a talk.

I need to make sure that we're okay.

But when I find him, Hunter is fast asleep on the bed, snoring not so peacefully.

He's exhausted. Both physically and mentally. So, perhaps the best thing to do is bide my time over the next couple of weeks until after the fight is over, and then see how it goes.

I'm not usually a patient woman. But I want to support Hunter. I love him more than anything.

CHAPTER 17

~HUNTER~

"I could have brought Rach to you," I say as Dad and I walk behind the house, along the cliffs. It's become a favorite spot for all of us these past few months.

Especially during the past month since I accepted Danny's challenge. I've trained harder in the past thirty days than I ever have in my life. I'm in excellent condition.

I won't lose.

"You know your mother and I don't mind coming over here," he says and shoves his hands into his pockets. "We close on our place in a couple of weeks. We're eager to be here full time. It'll be easier all around, and your mother will stop complaining that her babies are too far away."

"You love it here," I say with a grin. "Don't deny it."

"You know I do." Dad's smile isn't the least bit shy.

"Maeve found us the perfect place, right on the water. You didn't have to buy it for us. We could have done it with the money from the sale of the Seattle house."

"I did need to buy it," I reply. "The money is nothing to me, Dad. You know that. I can never repay you for everything you've done for me."

"We're your family," he reminds me. "You don't have to repay us for a damn thing. We did what anyone would do. Rachel is a delight, and the light of our lives."

"You took us both in, when Rachel was born, without even blinking an eye."

"Of course, we did. If Rachel came to you in a similar situation, are you telling me you'd turn her away? Tell her to figure it out for herself?"

"Hell, no." I shove my hand through my hair. "I would do the same thing you did. But, Dad, you won't ever pay for anything again in your lifetime. Not if I can help it."

"We have plenty of money. You don't have to pay for every damn thing."

I shake my head and look out to the sea. It's churning with a dark mood that matches mine.

"It's already done. No takebacks." I laugh and then shrug a shoulder. "Maeve and I should be back in a few days."

"Are you sure about this?" he asks.

"Yeah. I'm sure."

"And if you get hit in the head again?"

I shake my head. "He won't get even one hit in. I'll

have him knocked out in less than ten seconds. He's an idiot for starting this. Everyone knows it. The odds in Vegas are ten to one in my favor."

Dad nods. "We'll be at the pub to watch the fight with the O'Callaghans."

"I figured."

"Boys!" We turn at the sound of Mom's voice. "Dinner's ready!"

"You always choose the fanciest hotels," Maeve says as we walk into the suite the next day.

"This one is comped by the resort," I reply with a satisfied smile. "Fighting in Vegas means we get some fun perks."

"Wow, I guess so."

Maeve sits on a couch and crosses her legs, watches me as I open a bottle of water and take a long sip.

"I'm worried about you," she admits.

"Why is that?"

"You've been…different this last month. I've chalked it up to seeing the professional fighter side of you for the first time because you were already retired when I met you."

"How am I different?"

"Stoic. Serious. Focused, yet distant. Do you realize that aside from sex, you've hardly touched me in weeks?"

I stare at her, stunned. "That's not true."

"Oh, it is. And I'm not complaining because I know this fight is important, and you *need* to be focused. If you're not, you could get seriously hurt, and I can't have that. Is this how it always was when you fought? Before? I asked Rachel and she said no, but maybe she just didn't realize it."

I frown and sit next to her, thinking it over. Was I always like that?

"I don't think so. I think it's just *this* fight. And I'm sorry if I've been distant. I don't mean to be. I don't want to forget anything. I need to keep my head in the game. I can't fuck this up."

She slides over and straddles my lap. My hands immediately rest on the globes of her perfect ass under the soft material of her dress.

"You're not going to fuck it up." Her voice is strong and sure. I love the confidence I hear from her. I can't even begin to tell her how much her support has meant to me over the past several weeks. "You're going to kick this dude's ass, and then we're going to get on with our lives."

"Carla really did file a lawsuit. She's trying to get custody of Rachel. I can't believe she pulled that shit, and it only makes me want to beat Danny's ass even more."

"The attorneys all laughed at the suit. It'll get thrown out. I feel awful because it seems this is all my fault."

"How in the hell could it be *your* fault?"

"You said it yourself." She threads her fingers through my hair in that way that both soothes and turns me on. "She's jealous of us. Of me. And I think that if I weren't part of the picture, she wouldn't have come around in the first place."

"Whether that's true or not, it doesn't matter. Because you *being* in the picture is the best thing that's ever happened to me. Well, besides Rachel, of course. That could be a tie."

She smiles and reaches between us to unzip my pants, unleashing my cock before sliding herself right over me.

"God, you fit like a damn glove," I murmur against her lips. She rides me at a steady, quick pace, her hands braced on the back of the sofa.

She's a fucking goddess. I can't believe I made her feel anything less than important and cherished while I trained for this fight.

I sit up so I can cover her mouth with mine. Our tongues tangle, and she moans, pushing down on me to ride out her orgasm.

"God, I love you," I groan and follow her over the edge.

She rests her forehead on my shoulder and fights to catch her breath.

"Marry me."

Her head pops up, and she stares at me with gorgeous, wide, green eyes. "What?"

"Marry me. Right now. In Vegas."

"Right now?" She laughs, but the smile fades when she sees that I'm perfectly serious. "Hunter."

"Maeve, I am so in love with you, I can't see straight. I want you, forever. And I want you now. But if you need all of the fancy wedding stuff with your family, I can wait. Not long, but I can."

She's shaking her head slowly.

"Is that a *'No, I won't marry you?'* Or a *'No, I won't marry you in Vegas?'*"

She climbs off my lap and hurries into the bathroom.

"Way to fuck that up, Meyers," I mutter and clean myself up. I hear the toilet flush, and then Maeve returns to the sitting area.

"Look, you can forget it for now. We can revisit—"

"It's funny," she interrupts, "because you always hear about the girls who have been planning their wedding in their heads for their whole lives. The flowers, the white dress, all the frills. My brothers all had gorgeous weddings. And it was nice, don't get me wrong. But that was never me. I don't need all the trappings."

She paces and then grins at me.

"You know our families will insist that we still have a big party to celebrate."

"Of course."

"My dad..." She turns to me with worried eyes. "He'd want—"

"I already talked to him," I assure her. "He gave me his blessing without hesitation."

She runs at me and launches herself into my arms. "Holy shit, we're getting married!"

"Is that a yes?"

She kisses me long and hard, and then giggles. "That's a hell yes! But your fight is tomorrow night. Do you want to do it before or after?"

"Before." I set her on her feet. "I want to do it *right now.*"

She blinks at me again. "We don't even have rings."

"Then we'd better go shopping."

Four hours later, I cross the threshold of the suite, this time with my bride in my arms.

"You're so old-fashioned," she says with a grin.

"That's me." I kick the door shut with my foot and carry Maeve straight back to the bedroom. But when I toss her on the bed and get ready to join her, she laughs and puts her hand up, stopping me.

The rock I bought her at Cartier sparkles in the sunlight.

"Wait. Before we do anything else, we have to call our families. Especially Rachel."

"You're right. Okay, Mrs. Meyers, let's call our girl."

I sit next to her on the bed as Maeve FaceTimes Rachel, who answers quickly.

"Hi, guys! Are you having fun? Is it hot there? Have you seen any famous people?"

"I hate to break it to you, but *I'm* famous people," I remind her and watch with humor as she rolls her eyes.

"*Real* famous people."

"You're grounded for that."

Rachel laughs, knowing full well that I'm kidding.

"How's work?" Maeve asks.

"It's good. Grandda says he's going to teach me to play chess sometime. And the baby is finally sleeping better for Izzy."

"Rach." I pinch the bridge of my nose. "We haven't been gone that long."

"What? She asked. Anyway, I have tonight off, so I'm going to Charity's house for dinner and a movie. But I'll be home at a decent hour."

I'm glad that she found a new best friend, one who's sweet and isn't obsessed with sex and finding beer.

It's been a nice change.

"We have news," Maeve says with a smile as she holds up her left hand.

"Oh, my God! He asked!"

"That's not all." I hold up *my* left hand, as well. "We went ahead and sealed the deal. Elvis performed the ceremony."

"Who's Elvis?" she asks. "Never mind. Yay! I'm so excited! Please tell me we can have a big party to celebrate. I can totally help with it."

"We definitely need a party," Maeve agrees.

"Awesome." Rach is running through the house, making me seasick. "Grams! Gramps! Dad and Maeve got married!"

We spend the next hour on the phone, calling all of the family and telling the story over and over again. No one is mad about us eloping. I thought maybe Maggie would be sad about it because she and Maeve are so close, but she was only excited, just like the others.

"Okay, that's done." I push Maeve back onto the bed after she tosses her phone aside. "Now, it's time for me to make love to my *wife*."

"Wow, I'm your wife." She grins and cups my face. "You're my husband. I'd rather not call you my hubby, if that's okay with you."

"Honey, you can call me whatever you want." I nip at her bottom lip just as the room phone rings. "Damn it, will I ever get you naked?"

"It could be something important," she points out and crawls to the side of the bed, retrieving the phone. "Hello, Mrs. Meyers speaking."

She winks at me, and I grin like a loon.

"Oh, sure. Okay, I'll let him know. Can it wait, or—? I see. Thanks."

She places the phone back in its cradle and sighs.

"They have something for you at the front desk. She said you're supposed to come down and get it."

"Why can't they just send it up?"

Maeve shrugs. "I don't know, I'm not psychic. She

said that it's important, and you have to go down right away."

"That's weird. Since when does that even happen?"

"Maybe it's perishable," Maeve suggests. "Maybe someone sent food or flowers. That's probably it. I bet my parents—or yours—sent something over in celebration."

"You're right." I rub my hand over my face and then stare at my gorgeous bride for a minute. "You're stunning."

"I'm not even in a wedding dress," she says with a laugh. "I guess jeans and a white blouse is the new wedding wear of the season. So chic."

"I think you look great." I crawl over and kiss her squarely on the mouth. "I'll be back in five minutes. When I get here, I want you naked and ready for me."

"That's not how wedding night sex works," she informs me. "Haven't you seen movies?"

I laugh and walk toward the door. "I'll see you in just a few."

I shut the door behind me, then walk down the hallway, whistling. My life is as good as it gets. Sexy wife, great kid, awesome home. I don't know why I've been so intent on this fight. On proving something to myself and the rest of the world.

Maybe it's because Danny basically called me a pussy on national television.

Of course, we all know that I'm no pussy.

But the image of Danny with his hands on my

daughter just played over and over in my head, and I know that I can't let him get away with that.

I turn a corner toward the elevator and am suddenly struck on the back of the head, falling to the floor.

I'm in and out of consciousness as a blurry face stands over me, a bat in his hands.

"Fuck you," he growls and hits me across the shoulders, kicks me in the stomach, and then strikes my head once more.

Everything goes black.

CHAPTER 18

~MAEVE~

I'm married.

I stare at the monster rock on my finger and grin.

I didn't expect to come to Vegas and get married pretty much the minute we landed. But what a fun surprise.

I'm also relieved that I talked with Hunter about how I've been feeling. I could see in his eyes that he didn't mean to distance himself from me. He's just so dedicated to winning this fight, it consumed him.

He more than made up for it.

I hurry into the bathroom and freshen up, trying to decide what I should put on for when Hunter gets back when the phone rings again.

"Did he forget something downstairs?" I wonder aloud.

I hurry over to answer.

"Hello?"

"This is the front desk. Is this Maeve, Hunter Meyer's companion?"

"I'm his wife," I reply with a frown.

"I'm sorry to inform you, but Mr. Meyers is being tended to by the EMTs on your floor at this time."

I hang up, not needing to hear another word. I rush out of the room and run down the hall, coming to a halt when I see at least six men in uniform standing around Hunter.

"What happened?" I demand and rush to them, but someone holds me back. "What happened to him?"

"Who are you?" the one holding me asks.

"I'm his *wife*. Who hurt him?"

There's blood. Too much blood.

"We don't know," he replies. "Another guest found him here, and we were called. We're going to take him to the hospital."

"Let me just grab my purse and I'll come with you."

"Yes, ma'am."

I run back to the room, grab my phone, Hunter's phone, my purse, and shoes, and then run back to where the EMTs already have Hunter on a gurney, lying down, his neck in a brace.

"He's not conscious," I'm told as I walk quickly next to him, holding his hand. "Someone beat him up pretty good."

"Jesus."

Everything moves quickly yet in slow motion at the

same time. We're rushed down the elevator and out to the waiting ambulance. Paparazzi are already waiting, their cameras up, photos snapping, but we're quickly hidden in the ambulance. With sirens blaring, we zoom toward the hospital.

The medics start an IV in Hunter's arm and hook him up to other wires and monitors.

"His pulse is strong," someone says. "Good blood pressure."

"He's going to have a hell of a concussion," someone else says, and I feel my stomach lurch.

The doctors warned him that he might not survive another concussion.

Oh, God.

I cling to Hunter's hand and pray, with all my might, that he makes it through this. That he regains consciousness and doesn't have any trauma from this injury.

What did they *do* to him? And who?

I have so many damn questions.

We arrive at the hospital in minutes and are rushed through the ambulance entrance to a small room where doctors and nurses are waiting.

"You can stay," I'm told briskly as they immediately get to work evaluating him, "but I need you to stand back out of the way."

I nod and huddle back in the corner, watching as they evaluate Hunter thoroughly.

"Ma'am?"

I turn to see a policewoman gesturing for me to come with her.

"While they do their thing, I'd like to ask you some questions."

"Of course." I follow her to a chair and sit next to her. "I don't know how much I can help."

"You'd be surprised," she says. "Tell me what you know."

I shake my head. "We got married this afternoon. We came back to the hotel to call our families and then got a call from the front desk. They said they had something downstairs for Hunter, and that he was to come get it right away. So, he did. That's the last time I saw him. The next thing I knew, they called to say that he was in the hallway, hurt. And then the ambulance arrived."

She nods, taking notes.

"Who would do this?" I demand. "He has a fight tomorrow night."

"We have a suspect," she says. "There is a security camera in each of the hallways and elevators in the hotel. We caught it on film."

"Holy shit, that was fast."

"He's Hunter Meyers," she reminds me. "The hotel was very cooperative. We don't think it was actually the front desk that called up to lure him down. We're still investigating, but I'll keep you posted. Here's my card. Feel free to call me if you remember anything else, or if you have questions."

"Thank you, Detective Perry," I reply, reading the name on the card. "Who is the suspect?"

She presses her lips together. "I can't tell you that until after we've made an arrest. I have men coming to stand guard. I don't want him—either of you, really—unprotected until we wrap this up. Which should happen in the next few hours."

"That's fast, too."

"This wasn't the crime of the century," she says. "I'll be in touch. Oh, and congratulations."

I hurry back to Hunter's room, just in time for the doctor to finish typing in his computer and look up at me.

"Are you family?"

"I'm his wife," I reply as I walk on stiff legs to Hunter's bedside. His head wounds have been dressed. He has bruises on his face and neck. Even on his arms. "What in the hell happened here?"

"I was going to ask you the same thing. From what I can tell, it looks like he was caught off guard and hit from behind. The head wound would have happened first. Then, when he was down, they kicked him around some more and did some damage to his face. The good news is, nothing is broken. He must have a damn hard head."

"You don't know the half of it." I link my fingers with Hunter's. "What's the bad news?"

"I have previous records here for your husband.

He's been seen in the same health system many times, mostly for head trauma due to his profession."

I nod and bite my lip.

"Even though there are no skull breaks, he suffered a pretty severe concussion."

"And his head was already fragile," I finish for him.

"It is. If he regains consciousness today, that'll be a very good sign. Unfortunately, the brain is still very much a mystery. Recovery, *healing*, is going to be up to him. But he's a fighter, and his vitals are strong. My money's on him. We're preparing a room for him upstairs, and we'll move him as soon as it's ready."

He nods and leaves the room. I'm left with relative quiet, just listening to the hustle and bustle outside of the room.

I kiss Hunter's hand and press it to my cheek.

"You'd better wake up," I say and feel tears drop onto my cheeks. "Damn it, Hunter, you'd better wake up. I didn't get married today just to turn around and be widowed. I need you. Rachel needs you. Our life doesn't work without you."

I kiss his cheek and whisper in his ear.

"I know you can hear me. I need you to *fight*, goddamn it. That's what you do best. You fight."

I hear a buzzing in my handbag. I reach over and pull out Hunter's phone which is buzzing with a call from his agent. Just as I'm about to answer, the medical staff comes in to move us upstairs, so I send the call to voicemail.

The move is quick, and once we're settled, I drop all of my things on the couch near the bed and scoot a chair over so I can sit with Hunter.

I have both his phone and mine on the bed next to me.

I don't know who to call first. I need to call his parents so they can talk to Rachel. I really want to hear my dad's voice.

But before I can make any call at all, Hunter's phone rings again.

"Hello," I say into the phone.

"What's going on?" Hunter's agent demands. "I saw media footage of Hunter getting loaded into an ambulance."

I give him a rundown of everything that's happened over the past couple of hours.

"Jesus fucking Christ," he growls.

"There's footage," I inform him. "The hotel has security footage."

"Good. I'm going to make some calls. Keep me posted on his condition. I didn't want him to accept this fight. I tried to talk him out of it."

"Do you think the attack has something to do with the fight?" I ask.

"It has *everything* to do with it. I'll call in a bit to check on him."

And then he hangs up.

I sigh, reach for my phone, and call my da.

"Well, hello there, my bonny lass."

"Da." I brace my head in my hand and hear the tears in my voice.

"What is it?"

I tell him everything I know in between bouts of sobbing and sniffling.

"Maeve, turn on the tele."

"What?"

"Keegan just turned on ESPN. You're going to want to see this."

I find the remote and turn on the TV, fumbling through channels until I find a news station covering the story.

"They're showing the security footage," I mutter, watching closely. "Oh my God, Da, that's Danny."

"Aye, it is. You need to call Hunter's father. You don't want Rachel to hear of this from the news."

"I'm calling him now. I love you, Da."

"I love you, too, me sweet girl."

I hang up and dial Jay's number, relaying all of the information once again.

"Jay, it's all over the news. It was Danny. It's plain as day on the footage."

"I have to get Rachel from Charity's," Jay says, urgency in his voice. "I'll get her and we'll get to Vegas as soon as we can."

"Give it a couple of hours to see how he does," I suggest. "I know you want to get here. But I'm hoping that we'll be headed home in a couple of days."

"I'm coming," Jay replies, no room for argument in his voice.

His son sounds exactly like him.

"Okay. Thank you, Jay."

I hang up, ignore both of our phones as they go crazy, and stare at the television screen as the news shows the footage over and over again and then cuts to the scene where Hunter and I are being loaded into the ambulance.

"Turn that shit off."

I spin without turning it off, surprised by the sound of Hunter's soft voice. His swollen eyes are open, and I reach for his hand to gently kiss his cheek.

"You woke up."

"You threatened me," is his only reply. "That fucker tried to kill me."

"He won't get away with it." I tell him about the evidence and then I hear from the television, "Breaking news. An arrest has been made in this case."

We watch as Danny and Carla are both led to police cars in handcuffs.

"This was maybe the busiest day of my life," I say and turn off the TV. "We got married, and then all of *this.*"

"We got married?" he asks.

"Oh, God. Did this mess with your memory?"

Hunter tries to grin, then winces. "Kidding. I remember making you marry me."

"You didn't make me." I kiss his cheek again. I can't

seem to stop kissing him. "I love you so much, babe. So, so much."

"Love you," he whispers. "Really tired."

"Let me call in the doctor."

I ring the bell and then watch as he's evaluated. The doctor smiles, then nods at me.

"This is a good sign," he says. "A *very* good sign. Hunter, I'm going to need you to really retire for good now, do you hear me?"

"Yeah." Hunter licks his lips. "I'm done. Have better things to do."

IT'S ABOUT ten o'clock at night. There's a light on over the sink across the room, but all of the other lights are out, casting the space in a soft white glow.

I've been sitting in this chair for the better part of six hours.

Hunter goes in and out of consciousness, but the doctor said that would be normal for tonight. They're monitoring him closely.

A shadow falls over the doorway, and I glance up to see Rachel standing there, looking longingly at her dad with tears in her eyes.

"Come here," I urge her and hold out my hand for hers.

She hurries around the bed and hugs me tightly,

clinging to me almost desperately, and then she sits on the bed at Hunter's hip and holds his hand.

"Daddy?"

Hunter stirs and opens his eyes, smiling when he sees his daughter.

"Hey, baby."

"Oh, Daddy." Rachel breaks down and lays her head gently on Hunter's chest. He circles the arm not attached to the IV around her and strokes her hair.

"I'm okay," he whispers.

Jay and Angie follow behind their granddaughter.

"We stopped at the nurse's station to ask some questions," Angie says and brushes her hand through Hunter's hair. "You scared us, my boy."

"Scared all of us," I agree.

"Danny and Carla are going to jail," Rachel says. "They were behind it all."

"Yeah," Hunter agrees. "I heard."

"When can you go home?" she asks.

"In a few days," I reply. "They want to keep an eye on him for a couple of days because of that head injury, and then we're free to leave."

"Good," Rachel says as Hunter reaches over for my hand. Even with a bruised face, he has a cocky grin on those lips.

"I'd like to introduce you all to my wife."

"Oh, my gosh, that's right," Angie says and hurries around the bed to give me a big hug. "Congratulations."

"Does that mean I can call you Ma?" Rachel asks,

surprising me. "You know, like you call Grandma? It's an Irish thing, right?"

I feel more tears fill my eyes. I would have thought I was completely out of tears with the number of them I've shed today, but it turns out I have a few more.

"Yeah, it is. And, yes, you can call me Ma if you want to."

"I want to," Rachel says as she hugs me. "Since it's official and all that."

"Why does everyone else get to hug my bride but me?" Hunter asks.

"You're so needy." I cross to him and kiss his forehead. He takes my hand.

"Yes. I am. I need you. I'll never stop needing you."

"Ew, if you're going to get mushy, we'll go to the hotel."

"Get used to the mushiness, stink bug," Hunter says and kisses my cheek. "Turns out, I'm a mushy man."

EPILOGUE

~MAEVE~

"Merry Christmas," I say to Rachel as I pass her a wrapped box with a big gold bow on top.

"I thought we already opened everything this morning," Rachel says with a frown as she accepts the box.

It's Christmas Day, midafternoon, and we're all gathered at my brother Kane's house to celebrate together as a family. Keegan even shut down the bar for the day. It's a busy place with new babies and plenty of laughter.

Even Anastasia's family is here.

It's a big party.

But Rachel and my da have been huddled together in a corner all afternoon. Da's been teaching her how to play chess on the new set she got for Christmas.

"There's one more to open," I reply with a shrug, and then grin up at my husband.

Hunter's injuries healed after several months of rest, and then some rehabilitation. I didn't think the bruises would ever fade.

Danny and Carla were both sentenced to prison time—Danny won't be out for years. It turned out that Carla was the one who originally called the room to have Hunter go downstairs. She was charged with aiding and abetting.

But we've all settled back into a groove here on the island.

"I won't say no to presents," Rachel says and tears into the paper.

There are two items.

A T-shirt.

And a set of keys.

"Whoa," Rachel says with wide eyes.

"You worked hard through driver's ed," Hunter says. "But before you make a mad dash for the driveway, read the shirt."

She holds it up and reads aloud: "World's Best Big Sister."

Her jaw drops.

"Are you *kidding* me?"

"No, ma'am," I say and laugh when she launches herself into my arms, then she signals to the others.

"You guys! My ma's gonna have a baby!"

"We know," Maggie replies with a laugh. "And let me tell you, it was a hard secret to keep."

"I'm always the last to know everything," Rachel

says, but the smile doesn't leave her face. "Can I see my car now?"

We follow her outside, and when she sees the little white Lexus with the shiny red bow, Rachel bounces excitedly on the balls of her feet.

"Oh my God, it's so *cute!*" She kisses her dad, hugs me, and then makes a mad dash for the car.

"Only you would buy a sixteen-year-old a luxury car," I say as we watch Keegan get in the passenger seat with Rachel so they can check it all out.

"I'm a car guy, babe. There was no way I was going to buy my daughter a Honda."

I laugh and then glance over to where Cameron and Maggie have their heads together.

Maggie rolls her eyes.

Cameron grins.

"I wish she'd talk to me about him," I murmur, and Hunter follows my gaze.

"Don't worry, he's figuring it out."

"How do *you* know?" I demand.

"I talked to him." Hunter shrugs like it's no big deal.

"You talked to him."

"Yep. He's sick of waiting, and he's got a good plan. There's no need to worry."

"You've just wormed your way right into my family, haven't you?"

"It's *our* family, babe." He kisses my cheek and then waves toward the Lexus as it pulls out of the driveway. "Our family."

. . .

IIF YOU ENJOYED Flirt With Me, you'll love Take A Chance With Me, coming January 25, 2022!

You can preorder here: https://www.kristenprobyauthor.com/take-a-chance-with-me

A FRIENDS TO LOVERS, soulmates story from Wall Street Journal and USA Today Bestselling author Kristen Proby, set in her beloved With Me In Seattle Series!

Cameron Cox has mastered the art of keeping secrets. His talent for computer hacking means he's been recruited for highly classified jobs since leaving the military. He travels the world, risking his life. But his biggest secret isn't from a government job or a foreign spy.

It's Maggie O'Callaghan.

He's loved her from afar, always standing by as the friend. He's been her rock through the hardest days of her life. But after his dangerous past comes crashing into his life and threatens the only woman he's ever loved, he has a choice to make.

Give up the secrets and win her heart.

Or watch Maggie walk away with his.

With more than twenty stories in the With Me In Seattle Series, I figured it was time to include a who's who in the world, listed by family. Please know this may contain spoilers for anyone who hasn't read all of the books, but it's a great reference for those who want to make sure they read about everyone.

The Williams Family

Luke Williams – Hollywood movie producer. Married to Natalie Williams, a professional photographer. Parents to Olivia, Keaton, Haley and Chelsea. {Come Away With Me}

Samantha Williams Nash – Professional. Married to mega rock star Leo Nash. {Rock With Me}

Mark Williams – Works in Construction, for Isaac Montgomery. Married to professional dancer

Meredith Summers. Parents to Lucy and Hudson. {Breathe With Me}

The Montgomery Family

Steven and Gail Montgomery – Parents of Isaac, Matt, Caleb, Will and Jules. Steven is the father of Dominic.

Isaac Montgomery – Eldest sibling. Owner for Montgomery Construction. Married to stay at home mom Stacy Montgomery. Parents to Sophie and Liam. {Under the Mistletoe With Me}

Matt Montgomery – Detective with the Seattle PD. Married to Nic Dalton Montgomery, the owner and baker at Succulent Sweets. Parents to Abigail and Finn. {Tied With Me}

Caleb Montgomery – Navy SEAL. Married to Brynna Vincent Montgomery. Parents to Josie, Maddie and Michael. {Safe With Me}

Will Montgomery – Quarterback for the Seattle professional football team. Married to Meg McBride Montgomery, a nurse at Seattle Children's Hospital. Parents to Erin and Zoey. {Play With Me}

Julianne (Jules) Montgomery McKenna – Entrepreneur. Married to Nate McKenna, the co-owner of their joint business. Parents to Stella. {Fight With Me}

Dominic Salvatore – Illegitimate son of Steven Montgomery. Owns vineyard and winery. Married to event planner Alecia. Parents to Emma. {Forever With Me}

Ed and Sherri Montgomery – Ed is Steven Montgomery's brother. Parents to Amelia, Anastasia and Archer.

Archer Montgomery – Eldest of the siblings. Real estate mogul. Married to Elena Watkins. {You Belong With Me}

Amelia Montgomery Crawford – YouTube sensation, makeup brand owner. Married to Wyatt Crawford, architect. {Stay With Me}

Anastasia Montgomery O'Callaghan – Wedding cake designer and baker. Married to Kane O'Callaghan, world-renown glass blowing artist. {Dream With Me}

The Crawford Family

Melody and Linus Crawford – Parents of Wyatt, Levi and Jace.

Wyatt Crawford – (Mentioned above) – {Stay With Me}

Jace Crawford – Best cardiothoracic surgeon on the west coast. Married to veterinarian Joy Thompson Crawford. {Love With Me}

Levi Crawford – Detective for Seattle PD. Married to mega pop star, Starla. {Dance With Me}

The O'Callaghan Family

Tom and Fiona O'Callaghan – Parents of Kane, Keegan, Shawn, Maeve and Maggie.

Kane O'Callaghan – referenced above. {Dream With Me}

Keegan O'Callaghan – Owner of O'Callaghan's Pub. Married to Isabella O'Callaghan, meteorologist. {Escape With Me}

Shawn O'Callaghan – Screenwriter. Married to Lexi Perry, novelist. {Imagine With Me}

Maeve O'Callaghan – Real Estate Agent. Married to Hunter Meyers. {Flirt With Me}

Margaret Mary O'Callaghan – Youngest sibling. Widowed. {Take A Chance With Me}

The Martinelli and Watkins Family

Vinnie and Claudia Watkins – Deceased. Parents to Elena Watkins. Vinnie is the former boss of the mafia syndicate.

Carlo and Flavia Martinelli – Carlo is the current mob boss. Parents to Carmine, Shane and Rocco.

Elena Watkins – Referenced above. {You Belong With Me}

Carmine Martinelli – Eldest son. Mafioso. {Underboss}

Shane Martinelli – Middle son. Mafioso. {Headhunter}

Rocco Martinelli – Youngest son. Mafioso. {Off the Record}

Other Important People

Asher Smith – Former partner to Matt Montgomery. Now lives in New Orleans, married to Lila Bailey, a college professor. {Easy With You, a 1001 Dark Nights Novella}

Bailey Whitworth, Gray McDermitt, Kevin Welling – {Burn With Me}

Benjamin Demarco – Owner of Sound Fitness, a gym in downtown Seattle. Married to Sabrina Harrison. {Shine With Me, a 1001 Dark Nights Novella}

Noel Thompson – Interior decorator. Sister to Joy Thompson. Married to Reed Taylor, a financial advisor. Parents to Piper. {Wonder With Me, a 1001 Dark Nights Novella}

NEWSLETTER SIGN UP

I hope you enjoyed reading this story as much as I enjoyed writing it! For upcoming book news, be sure to join my newsletter! I promise I will only send you news-filled mail, and none of the spam. You can sign up here:

https://mailchi.mp/kristenproby.com/newsletter-sign-up

Honor
Courage

Check out the full Big Sky universe here: https://www.kristenprobyauthor.com/under-the-big-sky

Bayou Magic
Shadows
Spells

Check out the full series here: https://www.kristenprobyauthor.com/bayou-magic

The Romancing Manhattan Series

All the Way
All it Takes
After All

Check out the full series here: https://www.kristenprobyauthor.com/romancing-manhattan

The Boudreaux Series

Easy Love
Easy Charm
Easy Melody
Easy Kisses
Easy Magic

Wicked Force: A Wicked Horse Vegas/Big Sky Novella
By Sawyer Bennett

All Stars Fall: A Seaside Pictures/Big Sky Novella
By Rachel Van Dyken

Hold On: A Play On/Big Sky Novella
By Samantha Young

Worth Fighting For: A Warrior Fight Club/Big Sky
Novella
By Laura Kaye

Crazy Imperfect Love: A Dirty Dicks/Big Sky Novella
By K.L. Grayson

Nothing Without You: A Forever Yours/Big Sky
Novella
By Monica Murphy

Check out the entire Crossover Collection here:
https://www.kristenprobyauthor.com/kristen-proby-crossover-collection

ABOUT THE AUTHOR

Kristen Proby has published close to fifty titles, many of which have hit the USA Today, New York Times and Wall Street Journal Bestsellers lists. She continues to self publish, best known for her With Me In Seattle and Boudreaux series, and is also proud to work with William Morrow, a division of HarperCollins, with the Fusion and Romancing Manhattan Series.

Kristen and her husband, John, make their home in her hometown of Whitefish, Montana with their two cats and dog.

facebook.com/booksbykristenproby

instagram.com/kristenproby

bookbub.com/profile/kristen-proby

goodreads.com/kristenproby